SHANNON in the SPOTLIGHT

KALENA MILLER

DELACORTE PRESS

Text copyright © 2023 by Kalena Miller
Jacket art copyright © 2023 by Maike Plenzke

All rights reserved. Published in the United States by Delacorte Press, an imprint of Random House Children's Books, a division of Penguin Random House LLC, New York.

Delacorte Press is a registered trademark and the colophon is a trademark of Penguin Random House LLC.

Visit us on the Web! rhcbooks.com

Educators and librarians, for a variety of teaching tools, visit us at RHTeachersLibrarians.com

Library of Congress Cataloging-in-Publication Data is available upon request.
ISBN 978-0-593-48605-4 (hardcover) — ISBN 978-0-593-48606-1 (lib. bdg.) — ISBN 978-0-593-48607-8 (ebook)

The text of this book is set in 12-point Sabon Next.
Interior design by Ken Crossland

Printed in the United States of America
10 9 8 7 6 5 4 3 2 1
First Edition

For all the kids who count
and check and clean—
you're okay.

SIXTEEN BARS

I stare at the ripped sheet of notebook paper taped to the auditorium door. There's a pen dangling from a string beside it and a line of kids waiting to sign up. Elise grabs the pen and scrawls her name at the bottom of the list.

"This is your chance, Shannon." Fatima prods me in the side with a sparkly blue nail and gives me a knowing look. She takes the pen from Elise and hands it to me. I shake my head, drop the pen, and watch it bounce back against the wall.

There are different levels of theater kids.

I'm a level one. I enjoy working on shows, but I'm mostly here for my friends. I'm a techie, which means I do behind-the-scenes stuff. It's true I sometimes envy the actors—singing and dancing is probably more fun than spending hours with a hot glue gun—but I stay where I'm comfortable. Standing alone onstage? Being judged by my friends? Performing for a packed audience? Those are the total opposite of comfortable.

Fatima is a level two. Like me, she prefers to work backstage. But while I'm partial to costume design and props, Fatima is obsessed with anything involving hammers and screwdrivers. Operating a power drill is her favorite hobby. She's talented too. Last summer, Fatima built a giant doghouse all by herself for our production of *You're a Good Man, Charlie Brown*.

Elise, the only actor among us, is a solid level three. She spends the week after auditions working on her prediction chart, a massive bulletin board where she guesses the entire cast list. Imagine a serial killer's lair with pictures and Post-it notes connected by bits of string. Except with more sequins.

"Are you sure?" Fatima asks. Kids are jostling behind us, but I stand frozen in place, staring at the list.

"Yeah, you should audition. You could be, like, a nun or something." Elise's words are supportive, but her voice is hollow. She's never said this out loud, but I know she enjoys being the only actor in our trio. Despite her fancy voice lessons, Elise gets insecure about her singing.

I take one more, slightly wistful, glance at the notebook paper, then shake my head. "Nope. I don't sing in public." That's my go-to excuse for avoiding the spotlight.

Nobody needs to know about the hours I spend under the covers watching videos of Broadway stars, imagining what it would feel like to be onstage.

Fatima sighs, disappointed by my decision, but Elise nods happily. She's jittery as we find seats in the darkened auditorium. We pick a row halfway back, near the other middle schoolers. As usual, I sit between my two best friends. Fatima is the kindest person I've ever met, but Elise's nervous energy on audition day stresses her out.

"Are we sure the song from *The Secret Garden* is right for me?" Elise's leg is bouncing up and down.

"Omigod, yes." Fatima sighs. "We've been over this a gazillion times."

"Okay." Elise chews on her thumbnail, and her shaking legs cause our entire row of auditorium seats to vibrate. I'm about to place one hand on her thigh to stop her trembling but then change my mind. Elise never complains when I'm acting weird.

That reminds me. I slide a tube of ChapStick out of my pocket and trace my lips in three complete circles. I press my lips together three times to evenly spread the waxy balm, then snap the lid back on.

My therapist would tell me to resist the urge to soothe my lips, but it's hard to fight my brain all the time. I know it's irrational, but I fear the entire day will be ruined if my lips get chapped. And with auditions today, I'm not taking any chances.

The noisy chatter filling the auditorium fades to silence as Mr. Bryant, the director of the Rosewood Youth Community Theater, walks onto the stage. A few rows behind us, Robert Zhang shushes everyone, even though the room is already quiet. (Yes, he's *that* kid.) Next to me, Elise's leg twitching intensifies as a dramatic spotlight shines on our director.

"Are you serious with that spot, Amir?" Mr. Bryant yells, squinting. "Come help with these packets."

In the back corner of the theater, Amir laughs and shuts off the light. Fatima groans. Amir is Mr. Bryant's star performer, personal coffee fetcher, and occasional substitute director. He's also Fatima's older brother.

"Welcome to the auditions for Rosewood Youth Community Theater's production of *The Sound of Music*!" Mr. Bryant gestures dramatically—because nobody in this room does anything *not* dramatically—while Amir fetches the stapled packets and hands them out, row by row. "While I'm excited to see so many returners, we also have some new faces," Mr. Bryant continues. "So let me explain how auditions will work . . ."

This is my third show, so I know the drill. Everyone auditioning will perform a thirty-second monologue and at least sixteen bars of a song. You're allowed to watch the other auditions, and even techies like me and Fatima can sit in the audience as long as we're quiet. Mr. Bryant only has two rules: No parents in the auditorium. And no Disney songs.

"Does that make sense to everyone?" Mr. Bryant asks, finishing his speech. There's a sea of nods, but nobody says anything.

Except for Elise, who whispers directly into my ear, "What about my monologue?" Her voice is frantic. "Maybe I need something with more emotional range? What do you think?"

My thoughts are that (1) Mr. Bryant usually checks his phone during the monologues, so (2) they can't matter *that* much, and (3) even if they do matter, it's too late for Elise to change anything now. Of course, I can't tell her any of those things.

"I love what you picked," I whisper back. "You don't want something too emotional."

Elise nods, but I can tell from the stricken look on her face I didn't help.

"All right! Let's get started." Mr. Bryant claps his hands, then heads to his usual table at the back of the theater. "Amir, you're first. Show everyone how it's done."

Amir makes a big show of turning in his signed permission slip, climbing onstage, and introducing himself. Fatima slumps farther into her seat, but I think it's sweet.

If I was auditioning for the first time, I would appreciate someone showing me what to do.

Amir gives the audience a half-smile, then rolls his shoulders back and closes his eyes. When he opens them again, it's like he's transformed into a different person. I don't understand much of the monologue, but a quick glance at Mr. Bryant tells me it's really good. Then, after another roll of the shoulders, Amir launches into his song. I don't have to be an expert to know his voice is spectacular.

"I think I'm in love with your brother." Elise gazes longingly at Amir as he exits the stage.

"Nope. No. Absolutely not." Fatima shakes her head. "That is unacceptable."

"Not as, like, a *boyfriend*," Elise says. "But as an artist. I'm in love with his talent."

"Yeah, that doesn't make it less weird," Fatima says, laughing.

I laugh, too, but I get what Elise means. If she's a level three theater kid, Amir is a level ten. He's devoted his life to making it to Broadway, and I think he's talented enough to do it. People from other parts of Minneapolis come to our shows just to see him perform. He's *that* good.

After Amir, the auditions get less interesting. Naomi Smith and Adeline Davis—both contenders for the lead role of Maria—sing the exact same song from *The King and I*, which causes a bit of whispering. Robert Zhang sings a mashup of two Ariana Grande songs. It's totally unexpected but kinda amazing. And two little girls named Riya and Sara perform an adorable song and dance routine to "You Are My Sunshine."

There is one kid who stands out—a newcomer named Micah, who introduces himself with an unsteady smile. Boys are rare in youth theater, but there's something extra special about Micah. When he performs his song from *James and the Giant Peach*, I feel like he's singing directly to me, Shannon Carter, in the twelfth row of the auditorium. Micah finishes with an awkward bow and jogs back down the aisle. This time, his grin is confident, and I look away before he notices me staring.

As the auditions continue, Elise's legs shake more and more violently. Her permission slip is clutched in one fist while the other hand grips the armrest so tightly her knuckles turn white. Fatima and I say reassuring things, but nothing calms her nerves. Finally, after what feels like a hundred auditions, it's Elise's turn.

"And last, but certainly not least, Elise Hoffman!" Mr. Bryant's voice booms from the back of the near-empty auditorium.

"Is it bad to be last?" Elise whispers as she stands up.

"Don't worry," I say. "You've got this."

Then, in my own little ritual, I tap each elbow three times. I don't know when I started the elbow tapping, but

7

it's something I've always done for good luck. I wouldn't call myself a superstitious person. It's more like an extra precaution. If Elise doesn't get cast, I don't want to feel like it's my fault because I didn't tap my elbows.

Amir whoops from the catwalk as Elise takes center stage. I had no idea he was up there, but Elise looks up and smiles. Her short hair, which she recently dyed bright purple, shines under the stage lights, and her maroon lipstick is a stark contrast against her fair skin. She rolls her shoulders a few times, like Amir always does, then begins her audition.

Fatima and I nod at each other in approval when Elise finishes her monologue. She didn't forget any lines or stumble over her words, which is usually her biggest obstacle. For her musical selection, Elise chose a sweet song called "The Girl I Mean to Be." I've been listening to her practice all week, but she's shakier than usual and her voice sounds strained. Fatima frowns at me and raises one eyebrow. I shrug in response. It isn't the greatest performance ever, but Mr. Bryant has known Elise for years. It's not like this is his first impression.

I give Elise an overly cheery thumbs-up, but she returns to her seat and buries her head in her arms. "That was so bad," she says. "I don't know what happened. I totally sucked. I can do so much better."

Fatima and I are used to Elise's postaudition dramatics,

but it's hard to be comforting when I kinda agree with her. Not about the sucking, obviously, but about it not being her best.

"I thought you were amazing," I say. "Seriously, I know you're worried about the song, but the monologue was so good."

Elise moans.

"Shannon's right," Fatima says. "And there are so many good parts in this show."

I make a face at Fatima. Elise has her heart set on being Brigitta, the middle von Trapp girl, so I'm not sure this is the best way to boost her confidence. But Fatima pushes forward.

"There are so many von Trapp kids," she says. "Or you could be a nun! You know they have the best singing parts."

"I guess." Elise sounds doubtful, but she lifts her head.

"Yeah, the nuns start the whole show," I say. "You know, like, 'How do you solve a problem like Maria?'" I sing in a high-pitched, melodramatic voice like the woman in the movie version.

Fatima joins in. "How do you catch a cloud and pin it down?" She's singing a full octave lower than me, and we must sound terrible together. But our enthusiasm is contagious.

Amir appears behind us and sings the next line. Then Robert Zhang jumps in. And Naomi and Adeline. Soon,

Elise is sitting and laughing and singing with the rest of us. More kids join, and Amir starts conducting with his hands, motioning for each of us to sing different lines in turn. When we reach the end, Amir points to me and I belt out the last line of the song as Naomi harmonizes.

"Who was that singing?" Mr. Bryant's loud voice startles me out of my giddiness. I had completely forgotten he was here.

"What did you say?" Amir yells back.

"Who sang the last line of the song?"

"That was Shannon," Fatima answers for me.

"Um, sorry we were loud," I say. "I . . . I thought auditions were over." My cheeks are hot and I'm stammering, but I can't help it. I feel anxious just thinking about someone being mad at me.

"Auditions *were* over. They're not anymore." Mr. Bryant emerges from the shadows and walks toward our little group.

"What are you talking about?" Amir asks. "Elise was our last person. I double-checked the sign-ups."

"What I'm talking about is you, Shannon Carter." Mr. Bryant points at me. "You were singing just now?"

I nod.

"Well, then." A smile tugs at the corner of his mouth. "Get up onstage. Because I am not leaving until you audition for the musical."

CENTER STAGE

I've been onstage before. Obviously.

I spend most of each summer on this stage, painting sets and playing improv games and listening to Mr. Bryant's motivational speeches. I even slept onstage once last year during a cast sleepover. But I've never been onstage like this.

With the lights shining so brightly I can only see the first two rows of the audience.

With everyone in the room watching me, waiting for me to act or sing or faint.

"I really don't sing." I hold up my hand to block the light, but I still can't see anybody.

"That's clearly untrue." Mr. Bryant's voice is confident. "You were singing mere moments ago."

"We were playing around," I say.

"Ah, play! The foundation of all theatrical endeavors."

I don't know how to respond, so I stay silent. I may not be able to see my friends, but I can feel their eyes. Are they angry with me? I know Fatima wanted me to audition, but we belong in the costume closet together, searching for hidden treasures and singing along to the radio. And Elise can't be happy to have more competition, especially after her disastrous performance.

Except you're not her competition, I remind myself. *You're a techie. You're not supposed to be here.*

"I'm not an actor," I say finally.

"Anyone can be an actor," I hear Amir say.

"Shh, don't make her nervous," Fatima whispers.

I'm getting overheated, but I can't tell if it's the lights or the pressure of standing onstage by myself. I shove a hand into my shorts pocket and grab my ChapStick. I apply three even coats, then smack my lips three times. I start to put the little tube away, but my lips suddenly feel dry again. I repeat the ritual. Three and three.

I've never explained this out loud, but something about the number three makes me feel safe. Would I survive putting on ChapStick just two times? Almost definitely. But when it only takes an extra second to reach the number three, why take that kind of risk?

"Nobody's forcing you to audition," Mr. Bryant says.

I roll my eyes. That's a blatant lie. Sure, there isn't

anybody holding a gun to my head, but peer pressure is legit. And I couldn't ignore Mr. Bryant and run away like a wimp.

"Okay, maybe I forced you a little." He laughs. "But seriously, Shannon. It's up to you. You have a great voice, so I'd love to hear you sing. But if you aren't interested, that's absolutely fine."

I wish Mr. Bryant had said those things before I climbed onto the stage. It's like riding a roller coaster. It's fine to skip the giant coaster altogether, but if you spend an hour standing in line and *then* get scared as you're being strapped into the seat, there's no way to chicken out without everyone seeing you.

I wipe my sweaty palms on my T-shirt. I feel the sudden, undeniable, basically irresistible urge to wash my hands. And the only way to satisfy that urge without running offstage is to complete this audition.

"Fine," I say. "But I don't have anything to sing."

"Do you know the song Elise sang?" Amir asks. "That would suit your range, probably."

"Um . . ." I know Elise's audition song by heart. Even if she hadn't been practicing all week, I've always loved *The Secret Garden.* Still, I can't sing the same song as my best friend. I don't want to accidentally upstage her. But I'm also not a person who lies. And I seriously need to wash my hands.

"Yeah, I guess so." I squeeze my eyes shut. I may not be able to see Elise's face, but I can imagine her horror. Someone else singing her song? That's a disaster. Or maybe I'll be terrible and make Elise look better by comparison.

"But what about a monologue?" I ask. "I didn't prepare anything."

"We've been debating whether or not you can sing for long enough," Mr. Bryant says. "I'm confident in your public speaking abilities." So I was right about the monologues not mattering. Which is not great news for Elise.

"Yeah, your emotional execution is top-notch," Amir says. "Very angsty."

"Shh, you're stressing her out!" Fatima whispers again.

"Let's hear you sing," Mr. Bryant says. "Whenever you're ready."

"Okay."

Part of me just wants to get through this audition. But another part of me wants to do more than survive. I've always believed I was a level one theater kid: here to support my friends and have fun over the summer. But maybe there's more for me than gluing feathers onto Styrofoam balls or making endless bags of popcorn at intermission.

It's not like anyone forced me onto the sidelines. That's always been my choice. The background is where I feel safe. The terror of standing center stage while everyone stares at me has always seemed overwhelming. But now that I'm up here with the lights in my eyes, I make a discovery: It's not as terrifying as I imagined. In fact, it's kind of exciting.

In the audience, Mr. Bryant clears his throat. "Anytime, Shannon."

Right. I need to perform something for this to count as an audition. I take a deep breath and wipe my palms across my denim shorts. I try to remember things I've heard about good vocalists. Stuff like projection, enunciation, and tone. Then I open my mouth and sing.

I know the words and the melody by heart, so I don't need to think about the song. Instead, I imagine I'm the character—a young girl who's lost everything and is trying to find herself again.

And then I'm not onstage anymore, but in the bedroom Mom and I shared back when we lived in our tiny apartment. I'm sitting cross-legged on my twin bed, counting the rosettes on my pillowcase. Mom is curled up next to me, stroking my hair and reading *The Secret Garden* out loud until I finally tire of counting flowers and fall asleep.

I don't remember singing the high notes at the end, but I must have. Because, suddenly, the song is over. The memory of Mom fades, and I'm back in the auditorium, standing center stage, grinning as my friends clap and cheer from the audience.

"Very nice," I hear Mr. Bryant say to someone, probably Amir.

I give a little curtsy, then hop off the stage. Before my eyes have even adjusted, Fatima is throwing her arms around my neck. "Omigod, Shan. That was amazing! I knew you would be great up there, but still. *Wow.*"

I shrug in response. I'm trying to play it cool, but I'm secretly super proud of myself. If someone told me this morning that I would be auditioning for the musical, I would have laughed in their face.

"Also, I was sitting next to Amir, and he was *very* impressed, not that he would ever admit it," Fatima whispers.

"You were great!" Adeline calls as she and Naomi leave the auditorium.

"So good!" someone I don't recognize yells.

I detangle myself from Fatima's hug and find Elise still sitting in our original seats. She doesn't say anything as I gather my purse and jacket.

"So, what did you think?" I ask timidly. "You wanted me to audition, right?"

"I mean, it wasn't really a *real* audition, you know?" Elise barely looks at me, and the happiness I'd been feeling turns to shame. I know I shouldn't expect praise from everyone, but Elise could have found something kind to say. She must know I'd been terrified up there.

"Well, yeah, I guess it wasn't." I don't know what else to

say. Even worse, I feel tears creeping into my eyes. I fumble with the pile of stuff in my arms, and my phone falls to the ground. I crouch down to retrieve it, thankful for the interruption. But as I'm reaching for the phone, my fingers graze the black carpet, and I freeze.

There's a dark stain a few inches to my left.

There are orange and brown crumbs littered up and down the aisle.

There's chewed-up gum stuck underneath the seat beside me.

I had been so ecstatic after my audition that I totally forgot to wash my hands. But my fingers just touched the filthy auditorium floor, and now the desire for antibacterial soap and warm water overtakes me. The dirtiness of the auditorium feels so intense—so scary, even—that I need to act this very moment. I shove my phone into my pocket and push past Elise.

"Sorry, bathroom," I say as I run out of the theater.

I blow past somebody in the lobby who congratulates me and pull open the door to the restroom. My heart is racing as I drop my stuff on the counter and turn on the faucet, sighing audibly as the water floods over my hands. I imagine dirt swirling down the drain, and the tension in my body releases. I take my time with the soap, lathering my hands in soothing circles—sets of three, as usual.

Fifteen minutes later, I'm totally refreshed and ready to

face the world again. I dry my hands with a paper towel and use my shoulder to push open the bathroom door. Mr. Bryant is waiting for me in the hallway.

"Hey, Shannon," he says.

"Hey." I look around the lobby, but everyone else is gone. That's not a surprise—my friends are used to me taking forever in the bathroom. Outside, I can see Mom's green Subaru waiting in the parking lot. She's also used to me being late, but I shouldn't dawdle much longer. I have therapy this afternoon. "What's up?" I ask.

"I wanted to check on you," Mr. Bryant says. "I was worried you were having postaudition nerves."

I wrinkle my nose. Did he think I was vomiting in there? "Nope," I say. "Just washing my hands."

"Great. Listen. I wanted to see how you were feeling. Obviously, your performance was spectacular. Your tone is so clear, and your interpretation of the song was haunting."

I don't really know what that means, but the rush of pride I felt right after the audition is coming back.

"I know you say you're not an actor, and I respect that," Mr. Bryant continues. "But here's the thing. I found out the Northern Repertory Theater downtown is *also* doing *The Sound of Music* this summer. What are the odds, right? *And* they're bringing in kids from Wisconsin. Now, I'm an educator first, and I shouldn't get competitive, but I need—"

"Okay, I'll do it."

"—the best possible cast, and you're part of . . ." Mr. Bryant stops midsentence and stares at me. "Wait, what did you say?"

"I said I'll do it. You don't have to convince me," I say. "I want to be onstage."

Mr. Bryant's mouth drops open in surprise, but he quickly recovers and offers me his hand. I don't do handshakes—after three years, Mr. Bryant *should* know this—so I give him a cheery thumbs-up instead.

Yes, I have a habit of telling adults what they want to hear. And yes, I need to leave this theater before I'm late for therapy. But that isn't why I agree to perform. When I was singing on that stage, I felt more alive than I have in years.

All I know for certain is I need to get that feeling back.

APPLE SLICES AND PEANUT BUTTER

"Hey, Mom." I throw my purse and jacket into the backseat.

"Hey, sweetie." Mom squeezes my leg as I buckle my seat belt. "Are you doing okay? I saw Elise and Fatima leave before you."

"I'm fine." I open the bag of apple slices left in the cupholder and retrieve my personal jar of peanut butter from the glove compartment. Apple slices and peanut butter are my go-to snack in the car.

"You sure?" Mom asks.

"Yup, I was just washing my hands so they left before me." I unscrew the jar and scoop out a glob of peanut butter with my apple. If Mom's in a good mood, she'll jokingly ask if I want some apple to go with my peanut butter. But this afternoon, she's quiet. One look at her wrinkled forehead tells me she's worrying.

"Only because I touched the floor," I say, not mentioning how desperately I wanted to wash my hands before the audition. I resisted that temptation, which means it doesn't count. "And I wasn't in the bathroom that long."

"Really?"

"Yeah, only a couple minutes."

Mom looks doubtful, but she doesn't push. Over the years, I've learned how to bend the truth just enough to soothe her worries without lying outright. It's a delicate balance, but I've had tons of practice.

I have a condition called obsessive-compulsive disorder, or OCD. Basically, my brain gets stuck on certain thoughts or worries (those are the obsessions), and I do a little ritual until the worry goes away (those are the compulsions). For example, being dirty feels *so* horrible, that my brain obsessively worries it will ruin my entire day—or week or month or year. So I wash my hands until I feel clean again. It seems like such an easy solution. Except the obsessions never actually disappear. They always come back, sometimes even stronger than before.

I can't blame Mom for worrying. She was with me in elementary school when the OCD was new and scary and uncontrollable. And she's the one who's there for me when I can't stop washing my hands or I need to be carried into my bedroom because my shoe got dirty. But most of the time, it's not so bad. I read about a guy with OCD who had to turn his lights on and off forty-nine times before leaving for work in the morning. Compared to that, my ChapStick thing isn't a big deal.

As usual, thinking about ChapStick makes me need ChapStick, so I put my apples aside and spread the balm across my lips. It's impossible to enjoy a snack with chapped lips. Mom is facing the road, but I can feel her eyes shift toward me.

"I promise I'll talk to Ariel about the hand washing," I say finally.

Mom sighs and her face relaxes. "That sounds great, sweetie."

Technically, my weekly therapy appointments are for me. To help manage the OCD. But I think Mom needs them as much as I do. She likes knowing somebody else is worried about my stuff too.

"Anyway, you'll never guess what happened at auditions!"

"What?"

"No, you have to guess."

"Okay." Mom steals one of my apple slices as she merges onto the highway. "Did Naomi and what's-her-name get into a fight over the lead role?"

"Her name is Adeline, and nope. They were both super good, though. It's going to be close."

"Let me think." Mom runs a hand through the long,

blond waves that fall halfway down her back. During the school year, Mom's hair is always pulled into a tight bun. She works as an administrator at the high school, so looking professional is important. But in the summer, she wears it loose. "I don't know," she says. "Did Amir force Fatima to audition or something?"

"Nope. But you're getting closer." I grin as I scoop peanut butter onto another apple slice.

"Just tell me, sweetie."

"Fine. The exciting thing is . . ." I start a drumroll on my thighs and wait until Mom joins in on the steering wheel. I suppose I shouldn't complain about Mr. Bryant being overdramatic. I'm just as bad.

"Your daughter, Shannon Marie Carter, auditioned for the musical!" I declare proudly.

"What are you talking about?" Mom asks.

I tell her everything. How I was tempted to add my name to the audition list but didn't. How Mr. Bryant overheard me singing and forced me onstage. How I was nervous at first, but then it was totally cool.

"Mr. Bryant said my voice was haunting," I say, reaching the end of my story. "But in a good way, I'm pretty sure. Not like a ghost or something."

I crunch on another apple slice as I wait for Mom to digest everything. But when she finally looks at me, her face isn't beaming with excitement, like I expected.

Instead, the crease in her forehead is back, and she's biting her bottom lip.

"Mom, what's wrong?" I offer her an apple, but she shakes her head.

"Nothing's wrong, sweetie." She tries to smile, but I see through her fake cheeriness. My mother is a terrible actor.

"Tell me."

"I'm concerned. That's all." Mom flips on her turn signal and takes the exit for downtown Minneapolis. I wait for her to continue. "What if this is too much, too fast. Obviously, I want you to do whatever makes you happy, but I worry. All those lines? All that pressure? It's a lot for anybody, especially someone with anxiety."

I sigh. My brain is complicated. The stuff that scares me doesn't always make sense. Things like being dirty and walking barefoot are terrifying. Sometimes I feel like a smudge of dirt on my palm could ruin my entire life. But roller coasters? Not scary at all. (Unless you count the mud on the handrails.) Snakes? My all-time favorite animal, especially the baby polka-dotted ones. Earthquakes and fires and tsunamis? Not nearly as frightening as losing my ChapStick.

I've tried explaining this to Mom, but she doesn't quite get it. She totally understands that dirt freaks me out. But in her mind, that means I should also be afraid of the big, normal-scary things. Like being in a musical.

"I'm telling you, I want to do this," I say. "I mean, I think I do."

"You *think* you do?" Mom asks.

"Mo-om. You're making me nervous. You should be saying stuff like, 'What part do you want?' or 'When is the cast list posted?'"

"Sorry," she says. "So, what part do you want? And when is the cast list posted?"

I groan. Mom reaches for my last piece of apple, but I grab it before she can. I'm fully coating the tiny slice in peanut butter when my phone buzzes. There's a new message in our group chat. My chest seizes with panic. I had been so worried about washing my hands that I totally forgot how weird Elise was acting. I quickly open the messages:

> **Elise:** Is your mom still taking us to Valley Fair tomorrow?

> **Me:** Yes!!!!

> **Fatima:** I was thinking. If Shannon can audition for the musical, maybe I can ride a roller coaster.

> **Me:** I'll believe it when I see it :)

Elise: Do you guys want to sleep over at my house after?

Me: Absolutely!!!

Fatima: YES.

Elise: Cool cool. My dads are having a party so there will be lots of food to steal.

Me: Ooh those crab things?

Elise: Ew those are gross but probably lol.

I send back a laughing emoji and frown at my phone. I thought Elise was angry with me, but she's acting normal now. She wouldn't be planning a sleepover if she was furious, would she?

I open my private text chain with Fatima. After three checks to make sure I'm not texting the wrong person, I start typing:

Me: Did you talk to Elise before you left?

Fatima: Yeah. Sorry I didn't wait for you. Amir was in a hurry.

Me: No worries. Did Elise seem weird at all?

Fatima: No. Why?

Me: After I got offstage, she seemed angry and not like herself.

Fatima: She was probably still upset about her audition.

Me: You're probably right.

Fatima: I feel bad for her.
Amir says it hurt her chances.

Me: That sucks. We can cheer her up tomorrow at Valley Fair.

Fatima: And eat all the crab things at her house.

Me: Yes!!!!

"Are you listening to a single word I'm saying?"

"Huh?" I look up from my phone and see we're sitting in the parking lot of my therapist's office. Well, technically we're parked in front of a ten-story concrete building.

Bonavich Behavioral Health occupies half of the fourth floor, and Ariel's office is in the back corner. "Oh, hey. We're here."

"We've been here for five minutes," Mom says. "Which you would know if you put down your phone."

"I was texting—" Mom's phone ringing cuts me off.

"Sorry, sorry." She looks at the screen. "Yes, I know I'm a hypocrite, but it's Grandma Ruby. I should probably answer." Mom glares at the phone as if that might make the ringing stop. She doesn't have the best relationship with her mother, and their phone conversations usually end with her stomping around the house and cleaning things that were already clean.

"Hello, Mother. Can you hold on for one second?" Mom starts to put her hand over the speaker. "No, I said wait. I'm dropping Shannon off at therapy. Can you please hold on? No, I'm—" Mom rolls her eyes at me, then points at the clock on the dashboard.

"It's fine," I whisper. "I'll go in without you."

"Wait, what's going on at your house?" Mom says to Grandma Ruby.

I'm opening the door when Mom grabs my arm. *Talk to Ariel about the musical,* she mouths. *And don't forget the hand washing.*

I know, I mouth back. Mom doesn't need to worry. Because if there's one person who thinks about my hand washing and ChapStick even more than I do, it's my therapist.

THERAPY

"How's your day been so far?"

"Good."

Ariel sits cross-legged in the armchair next to the window. As always, her leather shoes are placed by the door, and I can see her sock-covered feet sticking out from underneath her knees. Ariel always sits like this, and I've never been sure if she wants to seem more relatable or if she's an adult who genuinely prefers sitting crisscross applesauce. I keep the soles of my boots firmly on the floor. Every week, Ariel tells me to "get comfy" and "feel at home," but I can't imagine taking off my shoes in a public place. I have strict rules about shoe removal.

"You had your first play rehearsal today, right?" Ariel asks.

"It was auditions. For the musical. And I ended up auditioning, so that was unexpected."

On the wooden side table are a variety of little toys. *Fidgets,* Ariel calls them. A plastic Slinky, a Rubik's Cube, a ball of Silly Putty, and a little rubber crab. All of them are too dirty for me to touch—playing with them certainly wouldn't make me feel calmer—but sometimes I study the little crab when I don't know how to answer a question.

"Tell me what auditioning was like."

"Um, it went well." I'm suddenly not sure what else to say. I have no problem talking nonstop around Mom or Elise or Fatima, but something about being in therapy makes me quiet. I always feel like I'm being tested.

"Did you enjoy yourself?" Ariel asks.

"I was kinda nervous, but yeah. Now I'm not sure, though."

A couple months ago, when Mom said my new therapist was named Ariel, I laughed. *The Little Mermaid* was my favorite Disney movie, and I didn't know people were named Ariel in real life. So when I arrived for my first session and saw my new therapist, a pale woman with bright red hair, it was almost too much to handle. Even Mom thought the combination was strange. But Ariel—she pronounces her name *Ahh-riel,* unlike the mermaid—and I got along well, so we got past the weirdness. Still, when I stare at the grimy orange crab on her table, I wonder if Ariel is a hard-core Disney fan or if it's all a coincidence.

"What are you unsure about?"

"I don't know."

"Shannon." Ariel sweeps her red hair over her shoulder and leans forward, resting her elbows on her knees. "You can talk freely here. There is no judgment in this space. Just support."

I stare at my feet and bounce my fist against my thighs. Three times on the left. Three times on the right. I know Ariel is watching, but she doesn't prompt me further. Ever since I started seeing her, we've done this back-and-forth. I spend the first half of my session evading her questions, she eventually convinces me to talk, and then I tell her how I'm actually doing. I don't know why I waste her time with this nonsense every week, but Ariel doesn't mind. She says it's part of my process.

"Okay. Well, the director said I sang well, so that was cool. But after, I couldn't stop washing my hands. And then my mom made me worried about doing the musical. Like maybe I couldn't handle it because of the OCD."

"Do you think you can handle it?" Ariel asks.

"I want to," I say with certainty. "It felt good being onstage. It's hard to explain, I guess. I had all this energy when I was performing, and I almost felt like a different person. But maybe my mom is right, and it's not something I should do."

"Moms do tend to be worriers." Ariel winks at me.

"Personally, I think being in a musical would be an exciting challenge for you. Stepping outside of your comfort zone can be a powerful experience. There may be some bumpy patches, but we'll work through those together."

"Thanks, I guess." Mom will feel slightly better knowing Ariel thinks the musical is a good idea, but she'll still worry. She can't help herself.

"Now, you mentioned some trouble with washing your hands today," Ariel says. "Do you feel like the compulsions are getting worse?"

"I don't know." I'm back to staring at the crab.

"Sorry, that was a vague question." Ariel stands up, retrieves a notebook from a drawer in her desk, then returns to her chair. "Let me ask you this instead. How many extra times are you washing your hands each day? Not counting after you use the bathroom or before a meal. Just an estimate."

"I don't know." I fiddle with the hem of my T-shirt. "It depends on the day."

"Okay, let's talk about today." Ariel flips open her notebook. "Can you remember how many times?"

"Um . . . a lot today. But only because auditions were stressful."

"Shannon, my goal is to make your life a little bit easier." Ariel's voice is gentle, and I know she's telling the truth. Wannabe mermaid or not, she's the only therapist

I've ever really trusted. Way better than the bald dude who flirted nonstop with Mom or the horrible woman who made me cry.

"I know," I say in a small voice.

"I'm only looking for an approximate number," Ariel says. "It helps me know what you're going through. Take a minute if you need to."

I think back to the beginning of the day and count on my fingers. There was once right after I woke up. Three times while I was reading a book because I thought the ink was staining my hands. Twice during breakfast when my fork felt greasy. A few times while I was doing my hair and then a few more before driving to auditions. I'm barely to midmorning when I run out of fingers.

"What's the verdict?" Ariel asks.

"This is really embarrassing." I stare down at my hands.

"Shannon, there's zero judgment here, I promise."

"I know, I know. I guess . . . maybe twenty or thirty times?" I slump into the couch. Just because Ariel doesn't judge me doesn't mean I'm not judging myself. "But sometimes I just wash the palms of my hands, so my skin doesn't get too dry." That's mostly for practical reasons. If I added lotion to my hand-washing routine, I might never leave the bathroom.

"Hmm . . ." Ariel writes something in her notebook.

I glance around the room as she considers what our

new approach will be—therapists are always coming up with a new approach—but there's not much to see. Over time, I've discovered all therapists basically have the same office. An assortment of plush furniture, so patients have a choice of where to sit. Some sort of throw rug to hide the ugly carpet or linoleum that came with the office building. A bright lamp and drawn shades to obscure the time of day. And, of course, piles and piles of books about people like me.

I'm trying to see the books on the farthest shelf when I spot a fish statue nestled between two picture frames. It's squat and round, yellow with bright blue stripes, and has a big, goofy smile. I squint my eyes and it comes into clear focus. This cannot be a coincidence. Red hair, a rubber crab, and a statue of Flounder? Does Ariel actually think she's a Disney princess? There's no way she could get a job as a therapist if she was delusional, right? That sort of thing is usually the patient's job.

"Shannon, are you listening?"

"Sorry, I was distracted." I turn back to Ariel, and it's clear she's been talking at me for a while. Probably not the time to ask about her mermaid obsession. "What were you saying?"

"I was saying that I'd like to get a bit more proactive about addressing your OCD."

"Being here isn't proactive?" I don't understand. Every

week, I spend this hour in Ariel's office while my friends are reading or playing video games or doing literally anything else. That feels proactive to me.

"Well, we spend a lot of time talking," Ariel says.

And a lot of time staring at each other, I add to myself.

"Which is wonderful, of course. I'm always impressed by how well you understand your own needs." *She is?* "But there's more we can be working on together to address the parts of your life OCD makes difficult. Today, you washed your hands twenty or thirty times. When you started seeing me last month, you and your mom estimated it was around ten."

"Oh." I stare down at my knees. I can feel tears prickling at my eyes. I wouldn't necessarily call myself an overachiever, but I hate being bad at things. Whether it's pre-algebra, painting sets, or therapy, I like being above average. I'm not comfortable with the feeling of getting worse at something.

"I'd like to start working on some cognitive behavioral therapy," Ariel says. "Do you know what that is?"

I nod even though I'm a little fuzzy on the details. The last time a therapist wanted to do CBT, it was the scary lady who made me walk barefoot across her office until I was sobbing. I know Ariel would never try to make me cry, but CBT is definitely not a fun activity for summer vacation.

"How does that sound?" Ariel asks.

"Great!" There's no harm in lying if my therapist can clearly tell I'm lying, right?

"I know your world must be scary sometimes," Ariel says. "You've been dealt a difficult hand of cards." She's about to launch into one of her motivational pep talks, but she's cut off by my phone buzzing. I pull it out and check the caller ID.

"It's my mom."

"Go ahead and answer," Ariel says. "We're done for today. I'll talk to your mom about next steps, and we'll continue this next week."

"Thanks." I press the phone against my ear and hurry out of the room. "Hello? Mom?"

"Hey, sweetie." Her voice is muffled and I hear the faint sound of music.

"Where are you? Are you driving?"

"Yeah, I'm running a little late. There was an emergency at Grandma's house."

"An emergency?" My brain starts spinning. Emergencies are vague. And vague is bad. What if a stranger broke into her house? What if she was robbed? Grandma is a hard-core collector (dolls and stamps, mostly), so getting robbed would be devastating. My heart quickens at the thought of a burglar rummaging through her stamp collection.

"Shannon, listen to me." Mom's voice cuts through my panicked thoughts. "Your grandmother is fine. I promise. Hang out in the waiting room, and I'll be there in a few minutes, okay?"

I start to ask a million follow-up questions, but Mom doesn't wait to respond. The phone clicks off, leaving me alone with the scary sound of nothingness.

UNSPOKEN RULES

I hate the waiting room.

It should be reassuring, seeing other people here for therapy sessions. But I always wonder what these strangers are thinking. Can they tell I have OCD just by looking at me?

When I told Mom this worry, she assured me nobody was thinking about me. I don't believe her, though, because I know what *I'm* thinking about in the waiting room. I can't help but guess at why other patients are here.

Like the woman by the fish tank. She's wearing skinny jeans and a long-sleeve shirt that clings so tightly to her pale arms I can practically see her muscles. She's incredibly thin and her hair is dyed a brassy shade of blond. It's her choice of clothing that makes me wonder. Long sleeves on a hot day like today? Could be some sort of body image issue.

When our eyes meet briefly across the room, I take a quick breath and tap each elbow three times. If she's in a super dark place, I don't want to jinx anything by *not* tapping my elbows.

Sitting on the other side of the fish tank is an elderly man whose leathery skin is covered in sunspots and freckles. It's unusual to see older people—especially older men—in the waiting room. But this man seems super nervous. He's glancing around, fiddling with his watch, and inhaling sharply every other breath. I hope his session starts soon because he's getting more fidgety with every second. I tap my elbows for him and look away, out of respect. If I was having an anxiety attack, I wouldn't want anyone staring at me.

Next, my eyes find a boy with dark skin and a buzz cut who looks kinda familiar. He's about my age, maybe a little younger, and he's reading a comic book I don't recognize. Sitting beside him is an older Black man— I'm assuming his father—who's bent over a clipboard of paperwork. The boy seems happy, but he's got to be here for something. Maybe depression. One of my old therapists told me depression is dangerous because people get so good at hiding it.

I'm about to tap my elbows for the boy when he looks

up from his comic book. Our eyes meet and I startle. He looks familiar because he *is* familiar. Just hours ago, he was onstage dazzling the audience with his song from *James and the Giant Peach.* I jerk my head back toward the fish tank, but it's too late. The boy—his name is Micah, if I remember correctly—is grinning and waving at me.

I squeeze the armrests of my chair. I obviously recognize Micah, but I didn't think he would recognize me. I spent the afternoon sitting between Elise and Fatima in the dark auditorium. *Except for the fifteen minutes you spent onstage,* I remind myself. Micah must have still been around for my audition. I offer him a tight smile, then turn away. There are unspoken rules in the waiting room.

Rule number one: Don't talk to anyone other than the receptionist.

Rule number two: Don't sit right next to somebody if there are other seats available.

Rule number three: Don't make too much noise. If you need to cough or make a phone call, use the hallway.

I understood these rules from the moment I stepped into my first waiting room. Maybe it's because of my anxiety, but I wouldn't dare sit next to another patient or chat with a random stranger. But Micah seems to have no clue these rules exist. After a quick word to his dad—who *also* smiles and waves at me—Micah is striding toward me with purpose.

"Hey, Shannon," he calls while he's still twenty feet away.

Every head pivots to look at me. All these strangers are probably wondering how I know the weird boy who's disrupting the comfortable silence. I slump into my seat. Without asking permission or waiting for an invitation, Micah plops into the empty chair beside me. He's three for three. He's broken every single waiting room rule.

"Hey," I whisper quietly. Maybe Micah will take a hint from my volume and adjust his own.

He cocks his head to the side, then leans even closer to me. "Why are we whispering?" he asks, his breath tickling my ear.

I stare at him like he sprouted a second head. "Because we're in a waiting room?" I gesture to all the people who are quietly flipping through magazines or scrolling on their phones. "It's, like . . . a *thing*."

"Huh." Micah considers this information. "That's interesting," he says. "This is my first time here. My family just moved to Minnesota."

"Oh." It's not a very intelligent response, but there's too much information for me to process.

Does Micah mean this is his first time at therapy? Maybe he's getting a new diagnosis. That would explain his lack of awareness. Or is this simply his first time see-ing a therapist in Minnesota? A normal person would ask where he moved from, but Micah's eyes are preventing me from behaving like a normal person. They're a deep shade of brown—almost black, but not quite—and I can't stop staring.

"So, uh . . ." Micah laughs awkwardly and I tear my eyes away from his. My face feels hot as I stare at my hands. He must think I'm a total freak.

"I saw your audition while I was waiting for my dad," he says. At least he's speaking quietly now. "You were amazing. There was a girl in my old theater company who sang like you. Her voice was so clear and perfect. She got the lead in everything."

"Oh. Thanks, I guess."

Micah compared me to another girl. By *girl* does he mean girlfriend? I shake my head. I don't know why my brain jumped to that conclusion. I barely know this boy. I decide to ignore the girlfriend question and focus on the compliment.

"That's nice of you," I whisper. "I was really nervous. It was my first time auditioning." Micah's face lights up, and I realize those are the first real words I've spoken to him. I need to keep the conversation going. "So . . . uh . . . where did you move from?"

"Tacoma, Washington," Micah says. His voice is proud,

but I've never heard of Tacoma before. "It was cool. But my mom got a new job at the university, so we had to move."

"And you did theater in Tacoma?"

"Oh yeah. All the time."

That was the right question to ask because it gets Micah chatting about all the shows he's been in, the parts he's played, and how much he misses Heather—his *best* friend, not *girl*friend . . . not that I care about those things. As his voice gets more animated, it also gets louder. I don't mind *too* much. A few people glance in our direction, but nobody seems annoyed. I'm kinda glad to have the company.

We're debating whether the stage version or movie version of *The Sound of Music* is superior—the movie version is the correct opinion, obviously—when Mom walks through the door. Her blouse is untucked, and her hair is flying in a million directions. I shove my phone into my pocket and stand up. I need to get across the waiting room before Mom ends up talking to Micah. Now, *that* would be a disaster.

"My mom's here, so I have to go," I say.

"Oh, cool. Well, I'll see you at rehearsals," Micah says.

I make a face. "I might not get cast."

"After *that* audition? I wouldn't be worried."

"Or you might not get cast," I tease.

"After *my* audition?" Micah gives me a cocky smile. "I'm not worried about that either." He laughs and jogs back to sit with his dad. That boy still has no concept of waiting room etiquette. Ten minutes ago, I found that horrifying, but now it's endearing.

"Hey, sweetie," Mom says. I take her hand and drag her to the hallway as she looks over my shoulder. "Who's the boy you were talking to? He's cute, don't you think?"

"Mom, no," I say once we're out of the waiting room. "You don't get to call boys cute."

Talking to Micah, all my worries were put on hold, but now they come rushing back. My elderly grandmother. The mysterious emergency.

"What's going on with Grandma Ruby?" I ask. "Is everything okay?"

Instead of answering, Mom leads me to a couch in the hallway.

"Wait, is it bad? You're freaking me out."

"Okay, here's the deal." Mom folds her hands in her lap. "There was a fire at your grandmother's house."

"What?!"

"Let me explain," Mom says. "There was a small fire, which your grandmother thought she could handle by herself. Unfortunately, she's not a trained firefighter, and the house was damaged." Mom takes a deep breath. "Which means Grandma Ruby will be living with us for a while. She's in the car now."

"Living with us?" I try to imagine this. My entire life,

44

ever since my dad left, it's just been me and Mom. We never needed anybody else. When I asked Mom for a pet snake, she said our house was too small. Now we're going to live with another person? And not just any person, but *Grandma Ruby?*

"We'll both have to adjust," Mom says. "But it's not permanent. Only a couple weeks, hopefully. And who knows, maybe it will be fun sharing a room with Grandma."

"I have to share a room with her?!" I reach for my ChapStick. This is a whole new level of awful. I shudder as I imagine my grandmother's judgmental gaze following me to the bathroom every time I wash my hands.

"I'm sorry, sweetie. There's no space in my bedroom, and I can't put my mother on the couch. She can use your bed, and you can sleep on the trundle."

I nod, even though my trundle bed was supposed to be for sleepovers with friends, not for me while Grandma Ruby takes my bed.

"Thanks, sweetie." Mom kisses my forehead. "Did you know you're my favorite kid in the entire world?"

"I'm your only kid." That's what I always say.

"Still. I know you're the best." That's what Mom always says.

"So." There's a long pause. "Grandma's in the car."

"Yup." Mom claps her hands against her thighs and stands up. "And it's best if we don't keep her waiting."

LITTLE PUNKS AT THE FIRE DEPARTMENT

"The little punks at the fire department gave me bad advice." That's the first thing Grandma Ruby says. "They caused this problem, and they sure as hell better fix it."

"Mother, I'm serious." Mom glares at Grandma Ruby as she starts the car. "Can you watch your language around Shannon?"

"What? She's a teenager. You think she's never heard that before? I know how kids these days talk." Grandma Ruby cranes her neck to study me in the backseat. Her graying hair falls right above her shoulders, and she's wearing new eyeglasses—the giant speckled kind old ladies love. "How old are you?" It's the first time she's looked at me directly since I got in the car.

"Twelve," I say.

"Well, close enough." Grandma Ruby's eyes flit from

my messy ponytail to my faded T-shirt to my ankle boots. I try to look as small as possible. She makes a disapproving snorting noise, then turns back around.

Grandma Ruby is not your typical grandmother. She doesn't make cookies or babysit or send me knit sweaters on my birthday. She's never attended one of my shows, and she doesn't come to our house for dinner. Mom and I only visit twice a year—once on her birthday and once on Christmas—even though she lives in St. Paul, which isn't far at all. I used to envy kids who were close with their grandparents, but not so much anymore. Our infrequent visits are filled with terse conversation and shouting matches. Even if Grandma Ruby wanted to knit me sweaters, I'm not sure I would accept them.

"Are you ready for a life lesson, Shannon?" When she's not criticizing Mom, Grandma Ruby likes to share valuable life lessons with me. Stuff like, "Don't get married in Vegas" or "Don't mix multivitamins with red wine." They're amusing, but rarely useful.

"Sure," I say.

"Don't ever listen to the fire department." Grandma Ruby slaps her hand on the dashboard.

"That's terrible advice," Mom says as she stops at a red light. "Shannon, you should always listen to the fire department. *Especially* when your house is on fire." She glares at Grandma Ruby.

"Sure, listen to the fire department. They're excellent at destroying antique furniture and hardwood floors. That exquisite buffet table I found last year? Burnt to a crisp. I should sue them."

"Mother, you can't sue the fire department."

"Sure I can. They destroyed my property." Grandma Ruby snorts again and starts to light a cigarette.

"And you can't smoke in this car." The light turns green, and as Mom accelerates, she snatches the cigarette from Grandma Ruby's fingers and tosses it out the window.

"It's my body, Andrea. Are you telling me I can't put smoke into my own body? You're as bad as my doctor."

"You can do whatever you want," Mom says. "Just not in front of Shannon."

"She's twelve years old, for Pete's sake," Grandma snaps. "She knows what cigarettes are. Are you telling me your daughter—who is almost a teenager, by the way—is not intelligent enough to make her own decisions about whether or not to smoke?"

"Can we please get through a ten-minute car ride without you implying I'm stupid?" Mom's voice gets shriller with each word. "Or implying my daughter is stupid? Shannon is your granddaughter, if that means anything to you."

I press my nose against the window and try to ignore the bickering. Every once in a while, Mom and Grandma

Ruby get along perfectly. They'll spend an afternoon re-telling old stories and flipping through photo albums. But usually, our get-togethers go something like this:

Grandma Ruby criticizes Mom's job. Or her parenting choices. Or the graduate degree she didn't finish. Mom gets defensive and starts crying. I get anxious and disappear into a bathroom. Everyone pretends to be okay for a short meal, and then we go home early.

This is why we only see her twice a year.

"I'm doing you a favor here, Mother. If you can't respect—"

"Mom!" I cut her off midrant. "All the yelling is making me anxious, okay?"

I meet her eyes in the rearview mirror. I'm not exactly on the verge of a panic attack, but I know the threat of one will make her stop yelling. The car falls silent as Mom looks between the road and me. If we were alone, she would instruct me to take calming breaths, but we're not alone. With Grandma Ruby in the car, all she can do is watch with worried eyes.

"So what exactly happened to your house?" I turn to Grandma Ruby, who's now fiddling with an unlit cigarette.

"Ah, yes," she says. "My poor, poor house."

Mom sighs and pounds her fist on the steering wheel. Maybe asking about the house wasn't my best idea, but it's enough to distract Grandma Ruby. She twists around in her seat to face me directly.

"I was cooking a roast, and all of a sudden my oven caught on fire."

"Ovens don't randomly catch fire," Mom mutters. "You must have done something wrong."

Grandma brushes off her comment and continues talking to me. "Anyway, there was fire in my oven," she says, her voice growing more animated. "So I tried to put it out. I filled cups of water from my sink and doused the fire with orange juice and milk from my fridge. I used all the liquid I could find, and nothing was working. The fire was still burning."

"You tried using milk?" I feel bad for Grandma Ruby, but I can't help but laugh. The image of her dumping a gallon of milk onto a kitchen fire is both sad and hilarious.

"Nothing inside was helping, so I went to fetch the garden hose," she continues. "I sprayed water everywhere, but the fire wouldn't stop. So I gave up and called the fire department." Her voice is ominous. "*That* was my mistake."

"No, your mistake was not calling the fire department immediately," Mom says.

"Nonsense." Grandma Ruby turns back to me. "So I call the fire department, and do you know what they told me?" She waits for me to answer.

"Um, no?"

"They told me to leave the house right away!" Grandma Ruby yells so dramatically that Mom brakes in the middle of the street. Another car honks and another speeds around us.

"Mother, please," Mom says as she accelerates again. "You're going to get us killed."

"Can you believe that?" Grandma Ruby asks me, ignoring Mom entirely. Which, I must say, is better than yelling. "So I do what they say and leave the house, but the fire truck doesn't arrive for fifteen minutes. Of course, the fire is gone by then, but my house is flooded."

"Why is your house flooded?" I ask. Her story doesn't make any sense.

"She left the hose running," Mom says.

"And those little punks from the fire department didn't bother to turn the hose off!" Grandma shouts. "They let my house fill with water."

"Your house was probably flooded before they arrived," Mom says. "It's not the fire department's fault. You turned on the hose."

"The fire department can destroy someone's antique furniture and walk away like it never happened! Isn't that terrible, Shannon?" Grandma seems to expect an answer, but I don't know what to say. Thankfully, we're almost home.

"Yeah, I guess." Grandma Ruby scrunches her eyebrows

together, like she wants more from me. "I am really sorry, Grandma. That sucks about your house." She huffs a little, then turns back around.

"So, by your standards, Andrea, it's okay to say something sucks, but h—*h-e-l-l* is a bad word," Grandma Ruby says.

"Can we not talk about this?" Mom's voice is strained, like she's struggling to hold back tears. I have no clue how she's going to last two whole weeks with her mother. I don't see her lasting two more hours.

"I'm just saying, you're being—"

"Oh look, we're home!" Mom exclaims in a fake cheery voice as we pull into the driveway. The ride home from therapy only takes twenty minutes, but this particular trip felt like a century. Mom stops the car in the driveway and waits for me to climb out. She'll meet me at the front door.

"Why is Shannon getting out?" Grandma asks.

"Mother, you know she has OCD."

"So that means she can't be in the garage? Why must you coddle her so much?"

I slam the door shut before she can say more. Suddenly, my stomach feels queasy as I think about the other reason Grandma Ruby and Mom don't get along.

I must have been seven or eight, and Mom and I were at Grandma Ruby's house for our annual Christmas dinner. It was the beginning of my hand-washing phase, but before I started seeing a therapist. Dinner was on the table—roast duck, mashed potatoes, cranberry sauce, green bean casserole. Everything looked delicious, but I couldn't start eating until my hands were clean. I politely excused myself and went to the bathroom like I always did, but then I never came back.

After a few minutes, the yelling started. Mom was saying stuff like "It's just a habit" and "Let her wash her hands," but that made Grandma even angrier. She was screaming "This isn't normal" and "Your daughter needs help." I wanted to leave the bathroom and resolve the argument, but the fighting made me wash my hands more. It felt like an invisible force was keeping my hands under the faucet. That was the first time I remember not being able to stop.

I'm not sure how Grandma Ruby feels about my OCD these days. I'm pretty good at hiding compulsions when we're together, but I can't pretend to be someone I'm not in my own house. In my own bedroom. I take a deep breath and listen carefully as the garage door opens and then closes. If Grandma Ruby was mad back then, I can't imagine how she'll react now.

THREE PAIRS OF SHOES

I only wear three pairs of shoes.

Obviously, I own way more shoes than just the three pairs. I have a whole shelf in my closet dedicated to shoes, thanks to Mom. She's always been a shoe person. There are rubber flip-flops, black ballet flats, hiking boots that must be way too small for me by now. Brown suede booties with a short heel, high-top sneakers, rain boots covered in little yellow ducks. The few times I've allowed Elise and Fatima into my bedroom, they've been super jealous of my shoe collection. Keds, Nike, Converse, Doc Martens—over the years, my mom has spent way too much of her paycheck on shoes I will never wear.

At first, it was because she enjoyed buying me shoes and I enjoyed receiving them. Now, it's like she's testing me. She wants to see if there are any shoes cool enough or fancy enough for me to break the rules I've established for myself. I saw the receipt in the Nike bag. I know she spent $110 on sneakers half the girls in my grade would kill for. But I won't wear them. I can't.

I wear three pairs of shoes.

First are my outside shoes. They're black ankle boots made of fake leather with a zipper up the side. I found them at Target last year, and my feet haven't grown since then. I think they're a knockoff version of some fancy designer shoe, but that's not important. What I care about in a pair of shoes is comfort, cleanliness, and the speed with which I can pull them on and off my feet. My ankle boots are nice and squishy on the inside, the outside can be easily wiped clean with a wet paper towel, and the zipper means I can slide them on and off my feet in seconds. I would love to wear the Doc Martens or Air Force 1s sitting in my closet. But snaps, laces, buckles—that stuff gets in the way when you change your shoes as often as I do.

Next are my inside shoes, a pair of black-and-white checkerboard Vans. The pattern keeps me from obsessing too much about any flecks of dirt, but there's enough white for me to know with certainty the shoes are clean. These are also slip-ons, though they look a little silly over my typical ankle socks. But they're inside shoes, so that's okay.

Finally, I have my penguin slippers. These fuzzy slippers

are necessary because they keep me from worrying too much about any squished bugs or bits of food stuck to the bottom of my Vans. The penguin slippers are the final line of defense between my bedroom and the outside world.

It's the perfect system.

I enter through the front door, deposit my boots on the welcome mat, and slip into the Vans that are waiting on the shoe rack. I walk around in my Vans, get a snack, do whatever needs doing, then head upstairs. My penguin slippers are positioned right outside my bedroom, so I slide my feet into those and leave the Vans in their place. As the world around me gets cleaner, so do my shoes.

It was the perfect system. Until Grandma Ruby moved in.

Mom, Grandma, and I stand outside my bedroom door. It used to be Mom's room, but we switched spaces last year. My old bedroom was barely large enough for a double bed, and Mom said a girl my age needed a bigger room.

I take off my Vans and slide my socked feet into the penguin slippers, but I don't open the door. Instead, I stare down at Grandma Ruby's feet. She's wearing tan dress shoes with crisscrossed straps and short heels. The shoes are yellowing at the seams, and I can see dirt hiding in the cracked leather. These are not shoes I would normally allow into our house, let alone into my bedroom. Mom notices my panicked expression and nods at me in reassurance.

"Mother, could you take off your shoes, possibly?"

"Why would I do that?" Grandma Ruby looks appalled by Mom's suggestion.

"Well, this is Shannon's room, and she likes—"

"Oh, for Pete's sake." She kicks off her shoes and stands barefoot on the hardwood floor. Her bony feet are covered in purplish veins. I would prefer if she were wearing socks. Mom knows to wear clean socks in my bedroom, and I always loan my friends a pair if they come over in flip-flops. But I can't exactly ask Grandma Ruby to follow my shoe rules.

"Is that better?" Grandma Ruby wiggles her toes.

"Thanks, Grandma," I say, but my voice shakes and my throat goes dry when I imagine the soot and dust hiding on the soles of her feet.

Still, I manage to I turn the doorknob and walk inside. Mom busies herself with the trundle bed while Grandma Ruby pauses in the doorway. Her lips are pursed as she studies the surroundings. I don't know why she's judging my bedroom. It's pretty average: bed, dresser, mirror, bookshelf, desk. There are two framed pictures on the dresser—one with me and Mom, one with me, Elise, and Fatima—a scented candle on my bedside table, and some old gymnastics trophies on top of the bookshelf. Otherwise, the room lacks any personal touches. Mom has been bugging me about painting the walls or buying a pretty bedspread, but I like my bedroom plain. It looks cleaner that way.

"Shannon, can you get some sheets from the hall closet?" Mom asks.

"Which ones?"

"The blue ones, if you can find them." I hesitate. I prefer stark white sheets so I can know immediately if any dirt has contaminated them, but Mom shakes her head. "I washed the blue ones most recently. I promise they're clean, sweetie."

I stare at my white sheets and white pillowcases—the ones on the big bed where Grandma Ruby will be sleeping. "I want white ones," I whisper to Mom. "Please?"

She glances quickly over my shoulder at Grandma Ruby. "I'll clean the spare white ones for you tomorrow, I promise," Mom says. "Can you do blue for one night?"

I nod, and she squeezes my hand. Grandma is still in the doorway, so I slide past her and step into the hallway. I switch from penguin slippers to Vans and head for the closet. Behind me, I hear Grandma Ruby grumbling to Mom about something. She probably thinks I'm ungrateful for demanding different sheets. She wouldn't understand.

Sure enough, the light blue sheets are folded neatly in the hall closet while the white ones I was hoping for are crumpled in a dirty pile on the floor. There's no way I would let my body touch them. I return with the blue sheets, changing shoes and shimmying past Grandma Ruby once again.

"Perfect. Thanks, sweetie." I help Mom make the bed, while Grandma stands in the doorway, silently watching.

"Does this work for you?" Mom finally asks.

Grandma Ruby surveys my poufy white comforter, then nods.

"Perfect. Then I'm going to make us some dinner. Probably tenish minutes, okay?"

"Sounds good," I say.

Mom disappears downstairs, and I test out my new bed. The mattress is thin and it's weird being so close to the floor, but I'll make it work. It's not like I have a choice.

I try my best to get comfy and pull out my phone.

Me: Guess who moved into my bedroom?

Fatima: OMIGOD DID YOU GET A GOLDFISH TOO???

Me: No?

Fatima: Is it a cat? A dog? Please don't say it's a snake.

Me: I wish. No, my grandmother is moving in.

Fatima: ?????

Me: There was a fire in her kitchen. So we're sharing a room until her house is fixed.

Fatima: I have literally never heard you talk about your grandmother.

Me: I know.

I'm about to update Elise when Grandma Ruby clears her throat. "Sorry, did you say something?" I'm trying to be polite, but having an old lady hover in your doorway is super awkward. I was hoping she would go downstairs and help Mom with dinner.

"Do you have extra socks or slippers I could wear?" Grandma asks. "My feet are dirty, and I know that bothers you."

She lifts her leg and shows me the sole of her foot. I

gasp. Her wrinkled skin is covered in gray powder. It looks like chalk dust, but chalk dust that managed to get mixed with playground sand. I've never seen feet that dirty. I didn't know feet *could* be that dirty. It's my worst nightmare.

My throat swells and my heart starts to pound. Talking isn't an option, so I run for the dresser. I dig through my drawer of socks until I find some I'm willing to sacrifice— a pink, fuzzy pair I never wear because they make my feet sweat. I have to look away as she pulls them onto her disgusting feet.

"Thank you, Shannon."

"You're welcome."

Finally, Grandma Ruby steps inside my bedroom and starts unpacking her suitcase. I watch her sock-covered feet pad around the room and try my absolute best to not think about the filth hiding inside the fabric. The silence is awkward, but Fatima is right. I barely know Grandma Ruby. What am I supposed to say to her?

Soon, my closet is full of floral robes and lace cardigans. Perfume and makeup sit next to the picture frames on my dresser, and Grandma's stamp collection is displayed prominently on my bookshelf. This thing is growing more and more out of control. All I can do is lie on my trundle bed, scroll through my phone, and watch as my bedroom turns into a place I don't recognize. A place that definitely doesn't feel like home.

VALLEY FAIR

Celebrating the beginning of summer with roller coasters has been our tradition since elementary school. Every year, Mom drives me, Elise, and Fatima to Valley Fair, the amusement park outside of Minneapolis. Once we're inside the gates, Mom finds a shady bench to read while the three of us race against the sun to get on every single ride in the park. Well, Elise and I go on every ride. Fatima is scared of heights, spinning, and falling, so she sticks to the merry-go-round. On a horse that goes up and down if she's feeling brave.

I imagined this year would be the same. I was expecting a full day of dripping ice cream cones, ridiculous selfies, and theater gossip. I was not expecting Grandma Ruby to insist on tagging along.

"You're not going to enjoy yourself," Mom had argued at breakfast. "It's hot and crowded and full of junk food."

"Nonsense," Grandma Ruby had replied. "This is a family outing, and I'm part of the family. I would love to meet Shannon's friends. I'm sure they're delightful."

Which is how I end up in the backseat, squished between Elise and Fatima, while Grandma Ruby sits in the front. She switches the radio from my favorite pop station to classical music, which is not quite the summer soundtrack I imagined. Still, the sun is beaming through the windshield, I'm covered in three layers of sunscreen, and my friends and I are ready for a day of thrill rides and cotton candy.

"Do you go to a salon to get hair that color?" Grandma Ruby asks, twisting around to stare at Elise.

"She wasn't born with purple hair, Mother," Mom says from the front seat.

"I'm aware of how genetics work, Andrea," Grandma Ruby says crisply. "I'm simply getting to know Shannon's friends. Isn't that what you want?"

Mom sighs and pushes her sunglasses up the bridge of her nose. She has—on more than one occasion, in fact—told Grandma Ruby she should bond with me more, but this isn't how either of us pictured that happening. Next to me, Fatima giggles while Elise beams at the attention. Hair dye is her favorite topic of conversation.

"I go to a fancy salon in uptown," Elise says. "My stylist specializes in coloring hair. She can do pastels, ombré, total rainbow hair—whatever you want. It's all about keeping your hair healthy."

"Fascinating," Grandma Ruby says. I haven't spent enough time with my grandmother to know if she's being sarcastic or not, but Elise seems pleased. "Now, Fatima. I hear you enjoy set design. Tell me about your plans for the upcoming production. Did you know I used to be an actress?"

And so the car ride continues. Grandma Ruby switches between my friends, asking them insightful questions and commenting on their responses. I relax in my seat, enjoying the easy conversation. Even Mom seems content to have her mother along for the road trip. By the time we arrive at the amusement park and purchase five day passes, we've discussed famous Broadway set designers, the best way to prepare macaroni and cheese, and the differences between freshwater fish and saltwater fish.

Mom and Grandma Ruby pick a table near the entrance while Elise, Fatima, and I get in line for the Tilter. It's a circular spinning ride, and today Fatima decides she's brave enough to try. It's a perfect warm-up for the scarier coasters farther into the park.

"I thought your mom and grandmother argued all the time," Fatima says as we climb into the metal egg and snap the safety bar into place. That's the one problem with visiting Valley Fair as a threesome. All the rides are made for couples, so we alternate who has to sit alone. Across the circle, Elise grins and waves as she locks into her own egg.

"They usually do." I grab the mini bottle of sanitizer from my purse and clean my hands before putting on three coats of ChapStick. Maybe some people would be scared of spinning in circles at fifty miles per hour. I'm way more nervous about touching the metal bar with my bare skin.

"Every once in a while, they forget about fighting for a few hours," I say. "This is a special occasion."

"How is it sharing a bedroom with— Whoa!" Fatima reaches for my hand as the ride jerks into motion. "Oh no. This was a bad idea."

"This was a *great* idea," I say, squeezing her hand in return. We spin faster and faster, and I can hear Elise whooping and hollering. Her enthusiasm can always be heard from across the park. I take one look at Fatima before scooting to the far side of our bench, just in case she needs to hurl. I may not be afraid of heights, but vomit touching my body might actually kill me.

"Hey, you're okay," I say.

Fatima nods, but her normally golden brown skin is developing a sickly green tinge and her death grip is cutting off the blood flow to my hand. I don't enjoy my friend's discomfort, but it's kinda satisfying to be the brave one. Usually I'm freaking out about something silly—dirt or shoes or bugs—and she's comforting me. It's nice to switch roles every once in a while.

After the Tilter, Fatima joins Mom and Grandma Ruby at a picnic table while Elise and I get in line for Wild Thing, the tallest roller coaster in the park. Being alone with Elise makes me nervous. I'm worried she'll be angry or judgmental again, and that's not a version of my friend I enjoy. But it's like her strange behavior yesterday is totally forgotten. We chat about our sleepover plans and ice cream flavors and how we both dream of going to Cedar Point someday. Her dads say it's the best amusement park in the whole United States, and we want to check it out together.

The topic of auditions doesn't come up until lunchtime. We meet Mom and Grandma Ruby at the retro-themed diner where everyone orders a cheeseburger except Elise, who decided last week she wants to be pescatarian this summer, and Grandma Ruby, who looks horrified by the fried food on everyone's plates. As if Mom didn't warn her about that exact thing this morning. Grandma orders a small Diet Coke and mutters something about having a tuna fish sandwich at home.

After a quick trip to the bathroom—I only wash my hands three times, which is impressive for me—I join my friends at the umbrella-covered table. Mom and Grandma Ruby sit on the other side of the pavilion. By some miracle, they're still smiling and laughing.

"I was telling Elise how Amir spent the entire night recording his audition song over and over again," Fatima says. I squirt three packets of ketchup onto my plate for the French fries, then take a massive bite of my cheeseburger. "He was filming himself for another tryout."

I steal a glance at Elise to see her reaction at the mention of auditions, but the smile on her face doesn't falter. Maybe I really was imagining the awkwardness between us yesterday.

"What else is he auditioning for?" I ask. "Surely he's not worried about getting Captain von Trapp."

"Of course not," Fatima says. "The video is for a pre-professional program in New York City. Only five high schoolers get selected every year, so it's a long shot. But he would get to meet real Broadway actors and work with famous directors. It's an amazing opportunity."

"That's so cool," I say.

Fatima nods, her face flushed with pride. Amir may annoy her 99 percent of the time, but she's still his number-one fan.

A fit of laughter interrupts our conversation. I look up, shocked to recognize Grandma Ruby's gruff tone. She and Mom are doubled over, completely hysterical, while they chuck fries at each other. A family of four carrying trays loaded with food stops to stare at their strange behavior. A toddler dressed in plaid overalls and a floppy hat points and giggles. I would be mortified if I weren't so shocked.

"Those two definitely don't hate each other." Fatima shakes her head and laughs. A warm breeze blows through the pavilion, sending straw wrappers and napkins flying. I secure our trash with heavy water bottles, and Fatima adjusts her blue hijab. "What were we talking about?" she asks.

"Auditions," I say, a bit too quickly. I look at Elise again, but she's totally unbothered. She's staring at my cheeseburger longingly, her own veggie burger untouched.

"Do you want some?" I ask, offering my tray to her.

"I can't. I shouldn't. It's so hard." She runs her fingers through shiny purple hair. "I mean, I hate the animal industrial complex. But I also hate tofu." Elise shoves a handful of fries into her mouth. "Anyway. You were about to say something about auditions."

"Yeah. What about your cast predictions?" I ask, feeling bold. "Do you have your bulletin board set up?"

"Oh, just you wait." Elise grins. "I've gone digital this year. It's less creepy, and a real time saver. I'll show you tonight." She pushes her uneaten burger away. "I'm ready to get back to rides. You guys good?"

"Absolutely." I stand up to throw away my trash, and I

already feel lighter. Elise is fine. Our friendship is fine. It was just my brain overanalyzing every conversation and inventing problems where none exist. I should mention this to Ariel next session. Maybe she has tips for shutting off my brain when it starts to get wonky.

Together, Elise, Fatima, and I tear through the park, trying to finish as many rides as possible before the four o'clock departure time Mom announced this morning. Elise and I hit three more roller coasters—with stops for ice cream in between, obviously—while Fatima takes pictures and promises she'll try a roller coaster *next* year.

We finish our afternoon on the Ferris wheel. This time, we don't give Fatima a choice. She climbs into the swinging car and sits between me and Elise, clutching our sweaty legs like her life hangs in the balance.

"Don't worry," Elise says. "You'll be the last one to fall out, so you can watch us plummet to our deaths first."

"OMIGOD, SHUT UP!" Fatima squeals.

Elise cackles and I give her a dirty look, but I find myself laughing too. As the wheel lifts us higher, Fatima starts to tremble next to me. I wrap one arm around her shoulders and squeeze tight. While Elise mutters reassuring things, I crane my neck in all directions, appreciating the beauty of the afternoon. I can see all of Valley Fair, the almost-full parking lot, and the water park next door. Beyond that, I can see the highway and the river and a couple different lakes. When we reach the peak, I imagine I can see the entire state of Minnesota, a patchwork of blue and green and brown.

I like roller coasters almost as much as Elise, but the Ferris wheel is my favorite ride in the park. Up here, the worries that plague me every day don't exist. The hand washing and the shoe changing and the ChapStick—those concerns belong on the ground, not up here in the sky. Up here, with my friends by my side and the entire summer stretched before me, I am invincible.

PREDICTIONS

That feeling of bliss disappears as soon as my boots hit the concrete. Fatima and Elise are busy planning activities for tonight, but all I can think about is the layer of sweat and grime coating my entire body. After years of Valley Fair trips, I should be prepared for this discomfort, but the excitement of riding coasters and hanging out with my friends distracted me.

"I need to shower," I announce once we're strapped into the car.

Before we left the park, I spent fifteen minutes washing my hands in a bathroom that reeked of sunscreen and corn dogs, and I feel even ickier than before. I reach for the baby wipes Mom keeps in the center console, scrubbing my arms and legs with the damp cloth, but that does little to ease my anxiety.

"Okay," Mom says. Her face is thoughtful as she pulls onto the highway. On my right, Fatima is half sleep while Elise scrolls through Instagram on my left. "What if I drop off Elise and Fatima, then run you home to shower? I can drive you to Elise's house whenever you're ready."

"That's great. Thanks." I relax as much as the cramped middle seat will allow and let my eyes flutter shut. My friends are used to my habits. Elise doesn't even look up from her phone, just nods in agreement. Grandma Ruby is another matter entirely.

"Why does Shannon need to shower?" She doesn't even lower her voice. I cringe with embarrassment, but neither of my friends react.

"Because we spent the day at an amusement park," Mom says. "Don't you want to shower?"

"Certainly, but I wouldn't make you take multiple trips. That's extremely inconvenient."

"Mother, we are not discussing this right now." Mom glances meaningfully toward my friends. "We are not discussing this *here.*"

"Whatever you say, Andrea," Grandma Ruby says with a huff.

As their fights go, this one seems little at first. But whatever love they had felt for each other at Valley Fair is gone, and they continue sniping quietly the entire ride home.

The whispered accusations turn to shouting as soon

as my friends exit the car. I shower quickly—well, quickly for me—and repack my bag, grateful to be spending the night away from their grown-up drama. I knew the happy family act at the amusement park wouldn't last forever, but I was hoping for a few more hours of peace.

Elise lives just fifteen minutes away from me, but it's a completely different world. In her neighborhood, the houses all look like mini-mansions, nobody parks on the street—it's actually against the rules, according to Elise—and a few families even have swimming pools, which seems silly in a place like Minnesota.

Mom drops me off in the circle driveway and waves goodbye as I head for the oversized double doors. I've got a toothbrush and change of clothes stowed in my back-pack, and I'm carrying a spare pair of slippers. Fatima and I used to bring sleeping bags, but we don't bother any-more. One of us sleeps on an air mattress while the other shares Elise's queen-sized bed.

I knock politely on the door, but nobody hears me. Judging from the number of cars in the driveway and the noise coming from inside the house, I'm guessing the party is already in full force. I decide to let myself in.

Rarely do I feel jealous of Elise's life. Do I sometimes wish I had a trampoline in my backyard? Obviously, yes. But Elise has me and Fatima over all the time, and I like the coziness of my own house. Still, on nights like this, when Elise's dads are throwing one of their massive parties and the house is full of well-dressed adults laughing and eating delicious snacks, I can't help but feel a bit envious. Mom rarely has friends over, and if she does, all they do is drink wine and watch *The Bachelor.*

I swap my ankle boots for slippers in the entryway and walk timidly into the living room. Luckily for me, none of the glamorous partygoers seem to notice the underdressed twelve-year-old in their midst. I'm almost at the stairs when I hear my name.

"Shannon," Elise whisper-shouts from the dining room. She and Fatima are peeking through the doorway like they're on a covert mission. I scurry over to them, my slippers sliding on the polished wood floor.

"Hey! I wasn't expecting this many people."

"Shhhh!" Elise's eyes dart around the busy room.

"Why are you shushing me? It's noisy in here."

"She's hiding from her dads," Fatima says.

"Yeah, I cannot spend the next two hours being reintroduced to all of their friends and hearing about how much I've grown." Elise rolls her eyes. "I know, I'm, like, a gazillion feet tall. Can we please move on already?"

"So why are we downstairs, then?" I ask.

"The food, obviously."

Elise, Fatima, and I grab two paper plates each and pile them high with fancy finger foods. There are the fried crab puffs Elise's foodie dad makes for every occasion, of course, but also tiny hamburgers, shrimp skewers, lemon squares, and little cups of fruit salad. I choose an assortment of everything while Fatima fills her plates exclusively with crab puffs. After a quick stop in the kitchen, where Elise steals an entire tray of brownies, we head upstairs.

"Your mom and grandma seemed to get along today," Fatima says through a mouthful of crab. The three of us have settled into our usual spots. Me in the hot-pink wingback chair, Fatima with her back against the floor-length mirror, and Elise sprawled among the twenty accent pillows on her bed. My friends are still wearing their sweaty clothes from earlier today, and I try not to think about all that dirt contaminating the pillows.

"Yeah, until the ride home," I say. "You slept through that part."

"So is she, like, a mean person?" Elise stuffs an entire brownie into her mouth, spewing crumbs all over her bedspread.

"She's not *mean*," I say, feeling kinda guilty. Maybe I've been complaining too much. "I guess she just has a strong personality. She's really stubborn. And my mom is the exact same but totally different."

"The same but different?" Fatima asks.

"I mean, my mom is stubborn, too, but in a way that clashes with my grandmother. Last night, they couldn't even agree on what temperature the thermostat should be." I take a bite of my mini burger and chew slowly. "They're not thrilled about living together. But hopefully Grandma Ruby's house will get fixed soon."

"Knock on wood," Fatima says, and Elise pounds on her wooden headboard as a joke. I seriously need the luck, though, so when my friends look away, I tap my elbows three times.

We're still chatting about grandparents—all of Fatima's live in Egypt and Elise has never met hers—when Mr. Hoffman knocks on the door and, without waiting for an answer, pokes his head inside.

"Just checking on you girls." He ducks under the string of fairy lights hanging from the ceiling. Elise may not share DNA with either of her dads, but everyone jokes that she gets her height from this Mr. Hoffman, not the other one. He's over six feet tall and has curly hair that makes him look even taller.

"Sorry about the noise," he says. "This thing won't go too late."

"The food is delicious," I say as Elise attempts to hide the platter of brownies behind her pillow.

"Well, I thought you might be thirsty." Mr. Hoffman produces three water bottles from behind his back. He hands one to me, then one to Fatima. "Especially with all those brownies you've been eating."

"I don't know what you're talking about," Elise says, though the chocolate crumbs on her cheeks give her away.

"Sure you don't." He tosses a water bottle in her direction. Elise shrieks and covers her head, but the bottle lands on the opposite side of the bed. "Well, I'll leave you girls alone," he says, ducking back out of the room. "You know where to find me."

"So where are your predictions?" I ask once we're alone again. With the cast list being posted next week, it's the topic we're all thinking about. And after chatting with Elise today, I'm reassured that any weirdness I felt was just my imagination.

"Your room feels empty without the bulletin board," Fatima says. "What are audition predictions without sparkly string?"

"You won't miss the string once you see the beauty of my spreadsheet." Elise climbs off her bed and grabs the MacBook plugged in on her desk. "I already have a draft. Come look."

Elise sits on the edge of her bed, computer on her lap. Fatima grabs a second plate of crab puffs and joins her, but I hesitate. Elise may leave crumbs on her own bed, but my fingers could still have traces of powdered sugar from the lemon squares or ketchup from the mini burgers. And if my hands are dirty, there's no way I can have fun.

"What's up?" Fatima asks.

I hold up my hands in explanation.

"Sorry, yeah. Go wash your hands," Elise says. "We'll wait for you."

I exhale and hurry into her attached bathroom. I turn on the faucet, squirt lavender-scented soap into my hands, and thrust them under the stream of warm water. If there's one thing at Elise's house I feel jealous about, it's the water pressure. The speed at which water explodes into her sink makes my own faucet feel like a drizzle. Thirty seconds later, I dry my hands on the plush hand towel and join my friends on the bed.

"Okay." Elise taps her keyboard and the screen lights up. A spreadsheet is already open. "These are my predictions so far, but I'm open to suggestions. I hope I have a shot at Brigitta, but I was horrible, so who knows."

"You weren't horrible," Fatima and I say in unison.

I skim the list, searching for my own name, but I don't see myself among the lead roles. My chest deflates the tiniest bit. I guess Elise wasn't impressed by my audition.

I mostly agree with her other predictions. Amir will obviously be Captain von Trapp, though I'm sure Mr. Bryant would cast him as Maria if he could sing soprano. Elise put Naomi as Maria and Adeline as Liesl, the oldest daughter, but those could easily be switched. Her own name is next to Brigitta, the von Trapp child with the best solo parts. Brigitta may be Elise's dream role, but I'm not sure her audition was strong enough.

"What about Shannon?" Fatima asks. As Elise scrolls, I search the list of potential nuns and Nazis and partygoers, but I'm not anywhere. There's no way my audition was *that* bad. Mr. Bryant called me haunting.

"Oh." Elise doesn't look up from the screen. "I didn't know you were really auditioning."

My stomach seizes, and I swear my heart stops beating for a second. That's the exact same thing she said after I got offstage. That it wasn't a *real* audition. My fingers reach for the ChapStick in my pocket. I can't believe I deluded myself into believing everything was fine.

"I don't know." Fatima's eyes dart back and forth between me and Elise. "It seemed real to me. What did Mr. Bryant say? I know he was sticking around after auditions to talk with you."

"He was?" Elise's voice is sharp. "What did he say?"

My friends are both waiting for an answer, but I stall for a few more seconds with my ChapStick. When I finally speak, my voice comes out all squeaky and high-pitched. "Not much. Um . . . he was asking if I actually wanted to be in the musical." Maybe I'm imagining it, but I swear I can see Elise's eyes narrow. "And I said yes. That I thought it would be fun."

"That's great," Fatima says tentatively.

"Yeah." That's all Elise says. Then, after a few seconds of painful silence, she hops off the bed and plugs the computer in. I take the opportunity to move back to my armchair. I need physical distance between me and the bed.

"What are you doing?" Fatima asks Elise.

"Well, the list is all wrong now." Elise grabs a brush from her dresser and starts pulling it through her hair, more forcefully than necessary.

"We can help you fix it," Fatima says. "That could be fun."

Elise doesn't answer. I shrug helplessly at Fatima. She looks as anxious as I feel.

Fatima tries again. "Or you guys can help me plan my half-birthday party. I want to do something really cool this year."

Elise stays quiet. My cheeks are burning, and I don't know what to do with my hands, so I shove them under my butt. If it were possible to die from awkwardness, I would be a full-on corpse right now.

Fatima pushes ahead. "It's the Friday before tech week, so we should probably plan something early. What do you think?"

"Definitely. I love how you celebrate your half-birthday."

My voice is stiff, but it's true. While Amir and Fatima are five years apart, they were born on the exact same date, which drives Fatima nuts. She always gripes about her brother being the favorite child, and sharing a birthday is too much for her. So a few years back, Fatima decided to celebrate on her half-birthday instead. Really, that just means she has two parties a year, but I'm not one to complain about extra cake.

"So what do we think?" Fatima asks. "Laser tag? That trampoline gym?"

"They both sound cool," I say, though bouncing up and down with a bunch of sweaty strangers seems more terrifying than fun. "What do you think, Elise?"

Elise pauses with the hairbrush midair. She breathes in and out, then rolls her shoulders back like she did before her audition. Finally, she turns to us, her face expressionless.

"Can we do this later?" she asks with a tremble in her voice. "I'm really tired. I'm going to bed."

THE CAST LIST

I've never been great at waiting, and thirty-seven minutes is a long time to wait. Sure, it's less than an hour. And sure, it may not be long if you're sleeping or reading or doing anything enjoyable. But if you're sitting in the backseat of a car, listening to your mom and grandmother squabble about contractors, and counting down the seconds until the cast list is posted outside the theater? Trust me, thirty-seven minutes is a long time.

We've been at Grandma Ruby's house all morning. Well, technically I've been in her driveway all morning. Mom and Grandma Ruby were meeting with contractors about fixing the kitchen while I opted to sprawl in the backseat of the car and play *Tetris*. I couldn't stomach the thought of all that soot and ash touching my shoes. But now they're back in the car and the debating has begun.

"I know it costs a little extra, but insurance is going to cover that," Mom says. "I think you should go with the first company. They had better reviews. It's going to take longer than we expected either way."

"I didn't like that man." Grandma Ruby waves her hand dismissively. "He was smug. And he was typing on his cell phone the whole time."

"He was using the calculator, Mother. It's not like he was texting his friends."

"He was still smug. There's nothing worse than a man who talks down to you." Grandma Ruby twists around in her seat. "You hear that, Shannon? Never trust a man who talks down to you."

"He wasn't trying to be condescending." Mom sighs. "You kept interrupting with your own ideas—"

"Which he should value because I'm the customer!"

I check my phone again. Thirty-five minutes until the cast list goes up. It's a twenty-minute drive from Grandma's house to the theater, which means we don't even need to leave for another fifteen minutes. Now I'm the one who sighs.

"Sorry, I know this is boring." Mom smiles at me through the rearview mirror.

"It's fine," I say. "I'm just worried about the list."

"Do you want to head out now?" Mom asks.

"No!" I say too loudly. "Sorry, being early is awkward. I can't wait in the car like I have nowhere better to be."

"You're waiting in the car right now," Grandma Ruby says.

"It's different," I say. "Here, nobody can *see* me waiting in the car."

"Did you know I used to be an actress?" Grandma Ruby asks.

I hope my silence will stop her from going on. It doesn't.

"I was in a stellar production of *Guys and Dolls* back in my prime," she continues. "The critics raved about us. One review said my performance was spellbinding." It's not the first time she's mentioned this particular show since she moved in. Or the second or the third. Of course, every time she tells the story, it gets more and more glamorous.

"Is the musical stressing you out?" Mom asks, ignoring Grandma Ruby entirely. "Because it's not too late to back out, you know."

"Mom. No."

Honestly, my number one concern is Elise. After our uncomfortable exchange at the sleepover, she went to bed at nine o'clock without saying another word. Once all the party guests left, Fatima and I watched TV downstairs, but it's strange to hang out in someone else's house when they're not around. We could barely even talk about Elise with her dads checking on us every two minutes. Still, Fatima convinced me Elise was just worried about getting a part after her not-so-great audition. And that makes sense. Not getting cast would crush her.

I check the clock on my phone again and tap each elbow three times.

"Please let Elise get cast," I whisper to myself, and tap my elbows again.

"What's going on, sweetie? Are you worried about getting a part?" Mom gets extra concerned when she sees me doing rituals.

"A little," I say. "I'm way more worried about Elise, though. She wants Brigitta so badly, and I don't know if she's going to get it."

I'd recounted every detail of the sleepover when I got home yesterday. Like me, Mom was concerned about Elise's behavior. She's always willing to discuss things like sleepovers and friend drama.

"I can't handle an entire summer of her being upset," I say. "It would be so awkward."

"Shannon," Grandma Ruby says, her voice sharp. "If you're going to be a star, people's feelings will get hurt along the way. Show business is brutal. As an actress, you can't let these things bother you."

"Seriously, Mother? She's not trying to be an actress.

She's just having fun with her friends." Mom turns around to face me. "Don't let anyone pressure you into doing the musical if you don't want to. It's *your* decision."

"Oh, I'm pressuring her?" Grandma Ruby's voice is sarcastic. "You're the one pressuring her to quit, Andrea."

I bite my lip. While I'm always going to be on Mom's side, Grandma Ruby kinda has a point. I *really* wish Mom would stop asking if I'm sure about the musical. I understood her fears at first, but now it's starting to get on my nerves.

"So you're criticizing me in front of my daughter now?" Mom's trying to stick up for herself, but her voice is shaking. I hope she doesn't start crying. That would make everything worse.

"Oh, for Pete's sake. There's no need to be so sensitive. I'm merely pointing out that you have a tendency to coddle Shannon." Grandma Ruby pulls a cigarette out of her purse, but Mom snatches it and drops it in the cup holder.

I bury my face in my hands. This is exactly the kind of arguing I don't like. Why wouldn't Mom let me stay home alone? I could have gotten a ride with Fatima and Amir. Why did she insist on turning this morning into family time?

"Who are you to criticize my parenting?" Mom's voice is stronger now. It's like all those years of resentment are spilling out of her. "You've been living in my house for three days," Mom continues, "and you decide you're the expert?"

"We have to go." My voice is feeble in the midst of their shouting. Nobody pays attention to me. "We have to go!" I say again, raising my voice. "The cast list is going up soon."

I lean into the front seat, putting my body between the two sparring women. They stop arguing, but the icy glares they're exchanging across the center console are almost worse.

Mom nods stiffly, then shifts the car into reverse and backs out of the driveway. Technically, we don't need to leave for another ten minutes. Now I'll have to wait in the parking lot, the exact thing I wanted to avoid. But anything is better than this.

We arrive at the auditorium late.

Grandma Ruby may get angry quickly, but she calms down even faster. Less than five minutes after the blowup, she was complaining about a headache and demanding coffee. So we spent fifteen minutes in the Starbucks drive-through getting a black coffee for Grandma Ruby, an iced chai latte for Mom, and a strawberries and cream Frappuccino for me. We rolled into the parking lot at exactly 1:12 p.m.

There's a crowd around the glass doors and even more people running from their cars to see the list. Both Mom and Grandma Ruby turn to face me. I take a noisy slurp of my Frappuccino, ignoring their eyes. In previous summers, I loved seeing the cast list for the first time. It was so exciting to congratulate everyone and imagine what the musical would look like onstage.

This is totally different. The butterflies I felt in my stomach this morning have turned into full-fledged knots. I can tell myself that whatever is on the cast list doesn't matter. That I've only cared about being in the musical for a few days. That I'll be fine either way.

But I can't make myself truly believe those things. Not when a single piece of paper will determine my fate. *And* Elise's.

"Is Shannon okay?" Grandma Ruby asks.

"I don't know," Mom says. "Why don't you ask her?"

"I'm trying to be sensitive. You're always saying, 'Oh, don't talk about that around Shannon,' or 'Shannon has anxiety, so don't say those things.'"

"Don't be absurd," Mom says. "I clearly didn't mean—"

"I'm fine, and I'm leaving!" I plop what's left of my Frappuccino into the cup holder and jump out of the car. The possibility of another argument is enough to get me moving.

My nerves grow with every step, but I avoid making eye contact with the kids walking back to their cars. I hear excited chatter and a few cheers. My heart skips a beat when my phone vibrates in my back pocket. Is Fatima texting to congratulate me? Or is it Elise saying her life is ruined? But I don't look at my phone. Whether it's good news or bad, I deserve to see it for myself.

I'm holding my breath as I push through the crowd to see the list.

Maria—Naomi Smith
Captain von Trapp—Amir Suleiman
Liesl—Adeline Davis
Friedrich—Robert Zhang
Louisa—Elise Hoffman

My entire body relaxes. Elise may not have gotten Brigitta, but Louisa is an incredible part. Any disappointment she feels will be brief. Getting a lead role in a Rosewood Youth Community Theater production is no small feat. I'm going to have an amazing summer with my friends, just like I wanted. I'm grinning to myself as I continue reading the list.

Kurt—Micah Johnston
Brigitta—Shannon Carter
Marta—Sara Tiwari
Gretl—Riya Tiwari

My name doesn't register at first. I fully expected to be in the list of nuns. But then I do a double take and stare in shock.

Brigitta—Shannon Carter

I gasp. Brigitta? As in Brigitta von Trapp, one of the best parts in the entire musical? Performed by Shannon Carter? As in me, the girl who never sang in public before last week?

I'm so ecstatic I think I might explode. I want to jump up and down and scream. I want to throw my arms around the girl next to me, an older teenager I've never seen before. I want to sprint back to the car and tell my family the good news.

If I thought this summer was amazing seconds ago, it is now undeniably epic. My best friend and I will be onstage together, playing sisters and singing some of the most famous musical theater songs in the world. It doesn't get much better than that.

FIRST REHEARSAL

Fatima and I walk into the auditorium together but immediately part ways. She goes back to the dressing rooms where the techies are meeting. Normally I'd be right next to her. We'd be joking about the cast list and debating whether to sign up for costumes or set design. But not this year.

I walk slowly down the aisle. Mr. Bryant is shoving papers into folders while yelling into his cell phone, and clumps of kids are scattered across the stage and in the audience. All of this is new to me, and I'm not sure what I'm supposed to be doing.

"Hey, Shannon." Amir jogs past me. He had stopped by the vending machine for a Mountain Dew. "Sign in on the clipboard, okay?" He points to the stage.

"Thanks. When do we—" But I don't get to ask my

question, because Amir is quickly swallowed by a noisy group of older kids. Instead, I find the clipboard and scrawl my initials next to the name *Brigitta von Trapp*. A shiver of excitement runs through me. It still hasn't quite sunk in.

I scan the room, but there's no sign of Elise. She didn't respond to any of my happy texts last night, and Fatima told me she wasn't feeling well. I hope she's not upset about the cast list.

I freeze next to the clipboard, unsure of my next move. I may know most of the people in the auditorium, but that doesn't mean I can actually sit next to them or start a conversation.

It's like that paralyzing moment in the school cafeteria when you can't find any of your friends. You have approximately two seconds to pick a seat before you look like a total loser and kids start pelting you with tater tots. (At least that's what happens in my imagination.)

All the high schoolers are sitting in a circle, so that's a no go. The cute little girls I recognize from auditions, Sara and Riya, are talking to each other, but I don't want to seem like a babysitter. Robert Zhang is sitting alone, but what on earth would I say to Robert Zhang? My two seconds have more than passed—and I *really* want to avoid the shame of flying tots—so I slide into the first empty seat I see. It's only when my butt hits the velvet cushion that I realize I sat down next to Micah, who is fixated on a comic book.

"Hey," he says, not taking his eyes off the colorful illustrations.

"Hey," I say back.

I'm tempted to jump up and find a different seat, but that would be unbelievably rude. Still, my forehead starts to sweat as I think about the last time I saw Micah. What if he judges me for seeing a therapist? Or worse—what if he wants to *talk* about our encounter at Bonavich Behavioral Health?

A few seconds later, he shuts the book and looks up at me. "Sorry, just finishing my— Hey! I didn't realize it was you." Micah grins. "I guess both of our auditions were okay after all. It's nice to officially meet you, *Brigitta.*"

I can't help but smile back. "And you too, Kurt."

In all my excitement about getting cast—and the worry about getting Elise's dream role—it barely registered that Micah will also be playing a von Trapp child. But now that he's next to me, smelling like soap and clean laundry— two of my favorite scents in the whole world—it becomes real. I'm going to be onstage with the cute boy from the waiting room.

"So we're siblings," I say, cringing the moment I hear my own words. I don't have much experience with boys, but referring to myself as his sister can't be smart. There's a pause, and I look around the room again to see if Elise has arrived. It's so much harder to make small talk with strangers—even cute strangers with sparkling eyes—than it is to chat with your best friends. But no Elise yet. I turn back to Micah. "So what are you reading?"

"*My Hero Academia*. It's my favorite manga." He puts the book in my hands, and I recognize it as the same one he was reading in the waiting room. Which makes me wonder once again—why *was* he in the waiting room?

"Cool." I hand the book back to Micah. "What's it about?"

As he starts describing a plot I don't fully understand, I study his face for any sign of anxiety or depression or other mental illness. Not that you can identify those things on a person's face.

Micah hasn't brought up our random encounter yet, but what if he mentions my therapy sessions to someone else in the cast? My best friends may know about my OCD, but casual acquaintances definitely don't.

I shake my head, physically pushing the bad thoughts from my brain. I don't know much about Micah, but he clearly isn't a jerk. He wouldn't embarrass me in front of everybody. Not that seeing a therapist is embarrassing.

"You can borrow it sometime, if you'd like." Micah is still talking about the book. I force myself to stop staring at him. Though his eyes are unusually pretty. In the warm glow of the auditorium, they almost seem to glitter. "I'll bring you the first one," he says. "Jumping in at number ten wouldn't make much sense."

"That's great, thanks," I say. "Listen, can you not tell anyone about seeing me at . . . you know . . ?"

"Of course!" Micah says, nodding fervently. I'm grateful he knew what I meant. "I would never." He mimes locking his lips and throwing the key across the auditorium. Micah may not have a firm grasp on unspoken waiting room rules, but he gets unspoken human rules.

I'm about to thank him when everything starts happening at once. Mr. Bryant stands up and motions for everyone to be quiet. An out-of-breath Elise drops into the seat on the other side of Micah. And there's a huge booming sound and shouts of "Watch out!" behind the stage.

"What's going on back there?" Mr. Bryant shouts. "Everything okay?"

"Yup." Fatima pokes her head between the curtains. "Mrs. Davis was having us move some old set pieces."

Evelyn Davis is Adeline's mother and Mr. Bryant's volunteer tech director. She enjoys hammering things almost as much as Fatima and isn't always the strictest when it comes to safety precautions.

"Be careful back there," Mr. Bryant bellows. "I'm talking to you, Evelyn."

"You're here!" I whisper across Micah to Elise. "I'm sure

you saw my texts, but congratulations! I'm so happy you got Louisa."

Elise doesn't look up from her phone. She probably didn't hear me with all the commotion, but an uneasy feeling creeps into my stomach. Louisa is basically the same part as Brigitta. And Elise had the entire night to adjust to the news. Is she actually upset enough to give me the silent treatment? Or what if there's another reason she's mad at me?

"All right, all right." Mr. Bryant claps his hands a few times. "I want everyone onstage in a circle. Grab a script, grab a highlighter. Text your parents and tell them you're here until we read through the entire thing, okay? I'm talking start to finish, people."

There's a flurry of movement as everyone crowds around the stack of folders and box of highlighters. I try to follow Elise to the far end of the circle—well, it's more of an oblong triangle—but she squeezes in between Naomi and Adeline. Alarms start going off in my brain as I sit down next to Micah. Things are definitely not okay.

"While we're reading through the script today, I want everyone to start understanding their characters. What are their greatest fears? What are their deepest desires? What do they eat for breakfast in the morning?" There's a bit of laughter at that one. "The point is, over the next two months, I want you to really think about what it means to be Captain von Trapp." He nods to Amir. "Or Maria Rainer." He points to Naomi.

"What about me?" asks Jeremiah, the blond teenager who was cast as Rolf, the young Nazi who Liesl falls in love with.

"Well, you're not actually turning into Rolf, right? I'm not into that method nonsense where you act like your character all day long," Mr. Bryant explains. "You're playing a role, and sometimes that role is a terrible person. You don't have to agree with someone to understand what motivates them. We'll talk more about that later, okay? For now, let's get reading."

There's a bit of chatter and script rustling and then we begin. It turns out today doesn't involve any singing—we're just reading every single line in the entire show. And there are a lot of lines, especially for the adult characters who talk way more than they sing.

For the first thirty minutes, I follow along with my elbows propped on my legs. I only have to leave the stage one time to wash my hands, a new record for me. And once my part begins, I'm fully invested. I like reading Brigitta's lines almost as much as I enjoyed singing during the audition. She's smart and independent and way funnier than I expected. And she says whatever's on her mind, which makes me think I wouldn't mind being a bit more like her. I'm beginning to understand why Elise had her heart set on playing this particular character.

Two hours later, Rolf and Captain von Trapp are having their intense showdown, and the entire family escapes into neutral Switzerland to avoid the war. There's a round of applause and a few whoops from Amir. I stretch my legs, which had fallen asleep a few scenes back.

"See, we're right on time," Mr. Bryant says as he gets to his feet. "Great job, everyone. Our first music rehearsal is tomorrow, but I want you to take these scripts home. Learn them. Memorize them. I need everyone off book in two weeks, okay?"

"Two weeks?" Naomi asks. "That's not very much time."

"It's the summer," Mr. Bryant says. "What else are you doing?"

A few people mumble responses like "sleeping" or "working," but Mr. Bryant is adamant. All lines will be fully memorized in fourteen days. I wonder if he's always this stressed or if the theater downtown doing the exact same musical has something to do with it.

"I'll see you tomorrow?" Micah asks me once Mr. Bryant officially ends rehearsal.

"Definitely." I'm straightening the edges of my script when I spot Elise, heading down the aisle. "Sorry, I've got to run." Even with me sprinting, Elise is already in the lobby when I catch up to her.

"Hey, hold on." I have to grab Elise's arm to stop her. "Why are you leaving so fast?"

"Rehearsal is over," she says.

"Well, yeah."

Technically, that's true, but Elise, Fatima, and I always leave together. I figured we would wait until the techies were done working to at least say goodbye. Elise is glancing at the door like she wants to bolt away from the conversation. If I'm going to confront her, it has to be now. I decide to channel my inner Brigitta and say exactly what I'm thinking.

"You're acting strange," I blurt out. "Ever since the sleepover. You're not responding to my texts. You don't sit next to me. And . . ." Elise is still eyeing the door. "And you're not even looking at me right now! What is going on with you?"

"Nothing." Elise's voice is empty. She's one hundred percent lying.

"Look . . ." Other kids are streaming into the lobby, so I have to keep my voice down. "Whatever it is, you can tell me. I'm sorry if I did something wrong or whatever. I don't get what's going on. Are you mad I got Brigitta?"

"No, that would be ridiculous." Elise sighs and runs one

hand through her messy hair. "Listen, Shannon. Nothing is going on. Okay?"

"But you're acting like—"

"I'm busy," Elise snaps. "I have the musical. I have other friends. We don't need to spend every second of the day together."

"But . . ." I look down at my boots. I don't know how to respond. Of course we don't *need* to spend every second together. We're supposed to *want* to spend time together. That's the whole point of being best friends. Unless something happened and we're not best friends anymore.

I take a shaky breath and look up, ready to say all of this to Elise.

But she's already gone.

ONE STEP INSIDE

"So yeah. I guess that about covers it."

Ariel looks stunned. She opens her notebook, closes it again, and then clicks her pen a few times. When she asked how I was doing at the start of our session thirty minutes ago, I'm sure she expected my usual answer of "fine" or "okay." Instead, she got a detailed recounting of my life since we last met.

Grandma Ruby moving into my bedroom.

Me getting cast in the musical.

Elise freaking out about whatever Elise is freaking out about.

"You've had a lot on your mind," Ariel says.

That's a true statement. Ariel is one of those therapists who says true statements and then waits for you to respond. Normally, that trick doesn't work on me. But I guess nothing about today is normal.

"Well, I would talk to my mom, but now my grandmother is always around. Today, they picked me up from rehearsal together and argued the whole ride home. And it's not like I can talk to my friends. Maybe I could text Fatima, but what if Elise said something bad about me? I don't want to cause more drama. You know what I mean?"

"Interesting." Ariel runs her fingers through her hair. It's curly today, which makes her resemble the cartoon mermaid even more than usual. "How does it make you feel when your mother and grandmother are arguing?"

"Huh?" Out of all the things I've been ranting about, Mom and Grandma Ruby are not my biggest priority. "Stressed out, I guess. It's super uncomfortable when they fight about me and I'm in the same room. I don't know. They got along so well when we went to Valley Fair last week. I wish they could be like that all the time."

"Hmm." Ariel puts her notebook on a little side table that looks like an actual tree trunk. She stretches out her legs, wiggles her toes a little, and begins to walk around the room. I wrinkle my nose at the sight of her bare feet on the grayish carpet. I understand logically that Ariel's feet getting dirty doesn't make my feet dirty, but I feel an uncomfortable tingling on the soles of my feet nonetheless.

"Hmm," Ariel says again. Now she's the one acting weird. She's not usually at a loss for words.

"What does 'hmm' mean?" It's the kind of question Ariel would ask me, and it makes her smile.

"It means I'm not sure what we should do with the rest of our time." She sits down again, tucking her feet back under her legs. "My plan was to start some cognitive behavioral therapy. We spend a lot of time talking, and I'd like to really address the compulsive behaviors that make your life difficult. But these are your sessions, Shannon, so I'll leave it up to you."

"What do you mean?"

"I mean, would you like to work on an exposure exercise or should we keep discussing your week?"

"Um . . ."

Honestly, I would prefer to brainstorm every possible reason Elise could be acting weird. But my appointments with Ariel aren't cheap, and I wouldn't mind having more control over some of my annoying OCD habits. Especially now that I'm in the musical. I can't be putting on Chap-Stick in the middle of a song. Who knows if they even had ChapStick back in World War II?

"I guess the exercise," I say finally.

"So much enthusiasm," Ariel says.

"Sorry."

"No, it's perfectly understandable." She smiles. "People

assume therapy is lying on a couch and talking about your feelings, but it can involve challenging work. Having reservations is natural."

"Thanks." I stare at the miniature crab. I'm tempted to fiddle with him—that's what he's there for, after all—but I would need to wash my hands. And leaving a therapy session about my hand washing to do some hand washing is slightly embarrassing. I tuck my palms under my thighs instead.

"All right, then. Let's get started." Ariel rubs her hands together, like she's about to begin a science experiment. Which, I suppose, she is. "Have you ever tried cognitive behavioral therapy before?"

"Yeah. It didn't go so well."

I think back to fifth grade when my therapist—I think her name was Taylor?—forced me to walk across her disgusting office without shoes *or* socks. I was crying the entire time, and all I remember is feeling like a freak. Like I was some broken kid who couldn't be fixed. I never saw Taylor again, obviously. After that incident, Mom developed a super intense process for selecting the best possible therapists.

"It can be tough," Ariel says. "One thing we want to avoid with exposure therapy is doing too much, too quickly."

I nod vehemently. I wonder if Ariel read my mind or if Mom told her about my disastrous session with Taylor.

"That's why I spend lots of time getting to know my clients first," Ariel says. "And I want you to tell me if you ever feel overwhelmed, okay?"

I nod.

"Now, let me ask you this. Do you still wear three pairs of shoes at home?"

"Yeah?" I don't like where this is going. I cross my arms, feeling defensive. "But changing my shoes isn't hurting anyone."

"I'm not asking you to get rid of your shoes." Ariel leans forward in her chair. "Though I appreciate you telling me where your boundaries are. Right now, I just want you to tell me about your shoe process."

"Okay." I talk through my three pairs of shoes, even though I've explained the routine a billion times before. Boots outside, Vans downstairs, penguin slippers in the bedroom. Periodic cleaning of each pair. Backup shoes hidden in cardboard boxes in my closet. I've got the shoe speech memorized.

"One question," Ariel says. "When you get upstairs, you switch from Vans to slippers right outside your bedroom door, right?"

"Yeah. I don't care which way they're facing or anything, though. I don't have that kind of OCD." I once read about a kid who needed everything in his bedroom to point north. He could never get homework done because he was constantly adjusting his pencils.

"Okay, so here's your assignment. Sometime before our next session, I want you to step into your bedroom *before* switching shoes. All you have to do is take one step inside. Then you can switch shoes. Got it?"

"One step inside?" I thought exposure therapy was supposed to be hard. Not walking-across-the-gross-carpet-until-you-sob hard, but somewhat challenging. I've accidentally stepped inside my bedroom without switching shoes before, and everything was totally fine. "Do I have to be barefoot?" I'm trying to understand Ariel's plan.

"Nope. You can wear your Vans," she says. "Just try one step before you change into slippers. Do you think you can do that?"

"Yeah, that sounds easy." Honestly, I'm a little insulted Ariel thinks putting one foot inside my bedroom is a difficult task. How in the world is this supposed to help me fight OCD?

"That's good if it sounds easy." Ariel scribbles the instructions in her notebook, then rips out the page. "I should warn you, though. Sometimes stuff sounds easy during a session, but then it's harder when you try at home. Anxiety is a powerful thing, so don't be discouraged if you don't succeed right away."

"I think I'll be fine." I take the sheet of paper from Ariel.

Last year, I got straight As in school. I can use a sewing machine to make a simple dress. Back when I did gymnastics, I could do a perfect roundoff back handspring. Taking one step inside my bedroom won't be a problem.

"Are you sure this is actual therapy?" I ask. "Not to be rude, but we could probably do something harder. Nothing too scary . . ." I shudder at the thought of my bare feet touching the ground. "But definitely something more difficult than taking one step in the wrong shoes."

"I'm sure, Shannon." Ariel smiles. "Let's start here and see how it goes."

●●●●●●

I arrive home to the smell of tomatoes and garlic and onions wafting out of the kitchen. Mom isn't much of a cook, so our house usually smells more like pizza and Chinese takeout than home-cooked food.

"Is that my girls?" Grandma Ruby calls from the kitchen. "I've got spaghetti and meatballs ready in five minutes! Plus garlic bread, a salad, and my famous peanut butter squares for dessert."

"She's in a good mood," I whisper to Mom as I switch shoes.

Let's hope it stays that way, she mouths back.

I went straight to therapy from rehearsal, so my arms

are full with my script, jacket, and water bottle. I hurry across the living room and run upstairs to drop everything off. When I reach my bedroom door, I pause.

My penguin slippers are waiting for me, but maybe I should do my therapy homework right now. I've never been one to procrastinate. And if I do this little task, I'll have good news to share with Mom and Grandma Ruby at dinner.

I take a deep breath, clench my script to my chest, and lift my leg. For a few seconds, my left foot hovers over the line—the line where dark hardwood meets light hardwood, where hallway meets bedroom. I just have to step inside once, and I'll be done.

My leg trembles as I struggle to balance with one foot in the air. My stomach clenches. My eyes twitch. I try to place my foot on the floor, but something stops me. My whole body wobbles, and I fall backward into the hallway.

It's embarrassing to fail on my first attempt, but I'll claim that one was practice. This is a super easy task. I can do it no problem.

I'm mentally preparing to try again when my phone buzzes. I rearrange everything I'm holding to retrieve my phone from my pocket. But when I open the text from Fatima, my script and jacket fall to the floor. Tears well into my eyes, and I lean against the wall to steady myself.

Fatima: Elise needs a ride to rehearsal tomorrow. I said we could pick her up after we picked you up. But she said "I need a break from Shannon." What's going on?

Me: I DON'T KNOW. She won't talk to me at all. And when I forced her to talk after rehearsal, she kinda said she didn't want to be friends anymore. I don't know if this is about me getting Brigitta or something else.

Fatima: I was wondering why I didn't see you guys after rehearsal.

Me: Yeah, sorry. I don't know what to do. Can you talk to her and find out what's going on?

Fatima: I don't want to get in the middle of anything. I feel like this is between you two.

Me: Can you at least tell me if she says anything? I can ride with my mom tomorrow.

Fatima: Sounds good. I have to go eat dinner.

My chest heaves with silent sobs as Fatima's text bubble disappears. Usually, we all talk in a group chat. Out of habit, I open our message thread. My last texts with Elise are from before the sleepover. Before everything fell apart.

I pick up my script and jacket, jam my feet into my penguin slippers, and walk into the bedroom. Who cares about Ariel's weird assignment? It doesn't matter compared to everything else in my life.

One of my two best friends isn't speaking to me, and I might have an inkling as to what's wrong, but I have no actual proof. Now, that's an actual problem.

MEMORIZING

'm not a person who lies.

I've really never needed to. I obsessively follow rules. I'm the kid who does the worksheet even when there's a substitute teacher and my friends are playing cards. I've always assumed lying would make me feel guilty, which would make me feel anxious, which would be bad. Very, very bad.

But I lie to Ariel at our next therapy session. It's not as hard as I thought.

I didn't plan to lie about completing the assignment. I meant to try again, but I honestly forget until I'm sitting in Ariel's office and she's asking me about the exercise. I instinctively say it went well. And when Ariel looks surprised and perhaps a bit suspicious, I backtrack and say it was difficult, but I managed. And that's partially true. It was difficult, and I know I *could* manage if I tried again.

I feel a tinge of guilt when Ariel congratulates me. But when she says my next assignment is to walk across my bedroom in the wrong shoes, the guilt goes away. I'll complete this new task—which also sounds super easy—and then have a clean slate. If only my other problems had such simple solutions.

※ ※ ※ ※ ※ ※

I arrive at rehearsal the next week holding on to a tiny sliver of hope that Elise will have forgotten whatever she was mad about. Maybe this was all a terrible misunderstanding, we'll be friends again, and eventually we'll laugh about this ridiculous argument.

The total opposite happens. It's like we were never friends at all. It's like she doesn't even know me.

Actually, that's not true. Elise acknowledges people she doesn't know, but she won't even look at me. It's like I'm a ghost.

Elise starts hanging out with Naomi, Adeline, and a handful of nuns. I always feel awkward talking to the high school girls, but Elise doesn't seem to have a problem with it. She and Naomi are constantly laughing about funny animal memes, and I even hear her chatting with Adeline, who's debating whether or not to ask out Amir. I smile and pretend her silence doesn't hurt me, but I can't stop my brain from searching for answers: *Why did Elise ditch me? What did I do wrong? Will we ever speak again?*

Because Elise claimed the girls, I'm stuck hanging out with the boys. I love spending time with Micah. He's a nice buffer between me and Elise when we're onstage, and he's a surprisingly good listener. I can't talk to him about my friendship woes, though, because (1) I don't want anyone eavesdropping, (2) especially Elise, who is usually standing on his other side, and (3) we're not *that* close. But Micah laughs at all my Grandma Ruby stories and tells me what it's like to share a bedroom with his sixteen-year-old sister. I try my best to include Robert too. Yes, he's annoying, but I know from experience that having nobody talk to you sucks.

I'm even seeing Fatima less. She signed up for sets, costumes, *and* lights—she's basically living at the theater. So when she offers to help me memorize lines at the park—something both of us used to do with Elise—I'm thrilled.

Mom is busy running errands, so I decide to walk. I prefer traveling by car in the summertime—blasting the air-conditioning makes me feel cleaner—but at least the park is only a block away. As I'm zipping up my boots, Grandma Ruby appears next to me wearing a straw hat and tortoiseshell sunglasses.

"I'm coming with you to the park," she says.

"It's really okay, Grandma." I straighten up quickly. "Mom lets me go by myself. I don't need a chaperone."

"I'm not chaperoning you." Grandma makes a confused face, like this is a ridiculous suggestion. "I had a stroke of inspiration regarding the sets for your show, and I must discuss my ideas with Fatima."

"Umm . . . okay?"

I don't know how to tell Grandma Ruby that Mrs. Davis already has the sets planned. Or that Fatima invited me to the park, not my grandmother-turned-roommate. So the two of us walk side by side down the street, Grandma Ruby chatting nonstop about the importance of harmony and balance in design and me avoiding the sidewalk cracks. That's a habit I picked up in elementary school when Tommy Markson said that stepping on a crack would break my mother's back. I know he was kidding, but spinal cord injuries simply aren't worth the risk.

When we arrive, I'm shocked to learn that Fatima is just as excited to see Grandma Ruby as Grandma Ruby is to see her. The two of them embrace before launching into a heated debate about mountains and mansions. I wander in circles around the playground while they draw shapes in the grass, feeling slightly bitter that my seventy-year-old grandmother is occupying Fatima's attention. I've already lost one friend this summer. I don't need Grandma Ruby stealing Fatima from me too.

I let them have their fun for about ten minutes before inserting myself into the conversation. "Okay, let's go." I try to shuffle Fatima toward the swings. "Grandma, we have to work on my lines."

"Fine, if you must," Grandma Ruby huffs. "Fati, we *must* exchange phone numbers, okay? I'm afraid Shannon doesn't have the same eye for design as you and I."

"No, no, no." I firmly tug on Fatima's T-shirt. She's having a hard time controlling her laughter. *"Fati?"* I ask once we're out of earshot. "You two have nicknames now?"

"Your grandmother is so adorable," Fatima says. "And hilarious."

"It's not quite so hilarious when you're trying to sleep, and she won't stop talking about the time she met Tom Hanks."

"She met Tom Hanks?" Fatima's eyes are wide. "Omigod, I want to hear that story."

"Later," I say. "I seriously need help with my lines."

While I've always been decent at remembering things like vocabulary words or state capitals, learning all of Brigitta's lines hasn't been as easy as I thought it would be. The girl talks a lot. There's one monologue in particular I can't seem to get right.

The park is crowded in the late afternoon heat. Sunburned children climb on playground equipment, noisy teens pretend to play basketball on the blacktop, and groups of moms huddle around strollers, gossiping and laughing. But the swings are empty, so Fatima and I perch on the hot plastic and rock back and forth. I hand her my highlighted script.

"Even Amir is struggling to memorize everything quickly," Fatima says. She flips the book open to the sticky note that marks the first scene at the von Trapp house. "Okay, start at the beginning?" She pulls her swing back as far as it will go, then launches into a graceful arc.

"Yup. My first lines are when Maria arrives."

"Okay." Fatima sticks her tennis shoes in the gravel to halt the swing. "Let me see. Maria says, 'You didn't tell me how old you are, Louisa.'"

"'I'm Brigitta. She's Louisa and she's thirteen years old. And you're smart. I'm nine, and I think your dress is the ugliest one I ever saw.'" It's one of my favorite lines, and it's easy to remember because it's almost exactly the same in the movie.

"Good. Then, 'Brigitta, you mustn't say a thing like that.'"

"'Why not? Don't you think it's ugly?'" I recite.

"Perfect," Fatima says.

"Shannon!" Grandma Ruby hollers from a bench next to the playground. I didn't realize she had settled there. "That line needs more sass! Brigitta is the spunky one. You sound like you're mourning a dead pet or something."

"I'm just memorizing," I yell back.

"She has a point," Fatima says to me.

"Don't start taking her side," I say. "I'll do the emotions later. Just keep going."

I have everything memorized until Brigitta's one-on-one scene with Maria halfway through the show. It's my character's big moment, when she reveals to Maria that the captain is in love with her. But I can't seem to get all the words right.

"Okay, um. 'Remember the other night when we were all sitting on the floor singing the "Edelweiss" song he taught us?'" I pause briefly like I would onstage, then continue. "'You laughed at him for forgetting the words. He didn't forget the words. He just stopped singing to look at you.'" I glance up at Fatima. "Is that right?"

"Close. It's supposed to be, 'After we finished, you laughed at him.' You forgot the first part."

I groan and twist my swing in a circle. I've been over this a million times. "Do we even need that part?" I ask.

"You have to say the entire thing correctly." Grandma Ruby stands from her bench and makes her way toward us, frowning as the tiny playground pebbles cover her sandals. Even thinking about how dirty her feet are getting makes my stomach churn.

"We don't need help," I say.

"This isn't some little improv show," Grandma Ruby says, ignoring my protest. "It's a work of art, and *your* job is to learn it perfectly. Do you think you know better than Rodgers and Hammerstein?"

"Technically, Rodgers and Hammerstein wrote the music," Fatima says. "Howard Lindsay and Russel Crouse wrote the script."

Grandma Ruby stares at Fatima. It's not often somebody has the guts to correct her, especially as calmly as Fatima did. In the moment of silence that stretches between us, I wonder if there's going to be an argument. But then Grandma Ruby lets out a snort and perches hesitantly on the third swing.

"I like this one," she says, pointing to Fatima. "This girl knows her stuff."

The three of us keep working on my lines as the sun dips lower in the sky and the mosquitoes come out. Fatima reads the other parts while Grandma Ruby tells me to be more assertive or excited or snarky. I have to admit her strategy of saying the lines with feeling makes them easier to remember, and by the time Amir arrives at the park to pick up Fatima, I'm totally memorized. I could probably say my lines backward if Mr. Bryant asked me to.

"This was super fun," I say as we walk toward the parking lot. "Do you want to do the same thing tomorrow? We don't have to work on my lines. We could just hang out."

"Oh." Fatima bites her lip. "Um . . . sorry, but I have plans with Elise tomorrow."

"Of course. I get it." I try to sound nonchalant, but the urge to cry burns at the back of my throat. "Another time."

"Totally." Fatima nods enthusiastically, then turns to leave.

"Wait . . . uh . . . one question." It's the same question I've asked Fatima every day this week. "Has Elise talked about me?" I understand my friend not wanting to get in the middle of drama that doesn't involve her. I would probably feel the same way. But I keep checking to see if Elise has revealed anything. Any clue as to why she doesn't want to be friends anymore.

"No, sorry." Fatima shakes her head. "I still think it'll get better." She says this every day, too, but her voice is getting less and less optimistic. Amir honks from his car.

"It's fine," I say. "You should go."

I gather my things from the playground, and Grandma Ruby and I trudge back home. She's humming contentedly after exchanging numbers with Fatima, her new bestie, but all I feel is a heavy sadness tugging at my chest. The afternoon was fun, but it would have been ten times better with Elise there.

And I have no idea if that will ever happen again.

THUNDERSTORMS AND TORNADOES

"Ouch. You're on my hair," Adeline says.

"You're on my foot," Robert responds.

"Well, then move your foot."

"Why don't you move your hair?"

"Robert, you just stepped on me!" I shout, scrubbing my throbbing fingers with hand sanitizer.

"Um, you guys?" Sara's little voice pipes up. "Riya's about to fall."

"I'm okay," Riya says, though she's hanging halfway off the bed.

This is our second day rehearsing a song called "The Lonely Goatherd," but our first day with the actual bed. The song takes place during a thunderstorm when all the von Trapp kids get scared and run to Maria's room. They hide under the covers and sing about goats until they're less afraid. (I swear it's not as weird as it sounds.)

Our current problem is the four-poster bed the set design team found on Craigslist. It's a double bed, which is fine for sleeping one or two people, but not great for holding eight singing kids.

"Evelyn, are we sure there's no way to get a bigger bed?" Mr. Bryant asks.

"You're the one who set the budget." Mrs. Davis is busy fluffing pillows while Fatima measures the distance between bedposts.

"I know, I know." Mr. Bryant paces in circles, studying the bed. We've been stuck like this for twenty minutes now. If we're going to get any rehearsing done, we need to get a move on.

"You're still on my foot." Robert's breath is hot on the back of my neck. I instinctively reach for my ChapStick.

"God, stop talking about your foot," Adeline snaps. "So are you *sure* you don't have a problem with me asking out Amir?" She and Naomi have been discussing their love lives all afternoon. No eavesdropping is necessary, considering we're sitting on top of each other.

"Ew, no." Naomi sniffs. "He's not my type."

"Don't say 'ew.' That's rude." Fatima points her measuring tape at Naomi. She may be horrified by the thought of Amir dating someone in the show, but the way she defends him is sweet.

"Sorry, Fatima. I meant I don't see him like that."

"Are you okay?" Micah whispers on my other side. "You seem . . . stressed."

"Huh?" I look at Micah, who's staring at my ChapStick. I didn't realize I was still spreading it across my lips. "Yeah, I'm good." I snap the cap on and slide the tube back into my pocket, jostling Robert in the process.

Being crowded on a bed with seven other people isn't the most comfortable situation, but I haven't gotten *too* freaked out. I kept my boots on, so it's not like my feet are touching anything dirty.

"Okay, people." Mr. Bryant claps his hands a few times. "Let's get started. We have to re-choreograph most of the number to make this bed work." Mrs. Davis and Fatima head backstage while the rest of us quiet down. "Now, let me see."

Mr. Bryant starts rearranging people, then shouts to Mrs. Davis that he needs a cushioned bench. Our entrances will stay the same, but the boys will sit on a bench next to the bed. Naomi and Adeline are supposed to lean against the bedposts while Riya and Sara lie at its foot.

That leaves me and Elise with our backs against the headboard. It's hard for her to act like I don't exist when we're sitting next to each other, but she's still trying. She studies the pillow, picks at her nails, checks on the little girls—anything to avoid looking at me. But when Mr. Bryant tells us to move closer until we're basically cuddling, totally ignoring me becomes impossible.

"Sorry," I say when I'm told to place one arm around her shoulders. While I desperately want to be friends again, nobody should be forced to touch someone who repulses them. The thought makes me blink back tears. Is Elise actually repulsed by me?

"It's okay," she says.

It's been three weeks since the cast list was posted and we started rehearsals. It's also been three weeks since Elise spoke to me. Maybe it's okay if we're not best friends anymore. Maybe eventually we can be two people who casually say hello and occasionally talk during rehearsal. For a moment, I feel relief. Then I realize the prospect of being acquaintances might be even sadder.

As Mr. Bryant starts messing around with thunder sound effects, I think about the first time Elise and I met. It was third grade, and Elise had just moved to Minnesota. Fatima and I had been friends since kindergarten, but we weren't in the same class that year. So when my teacher asked if I would be Elise's buddy and help her adjust to our school, I agreed. There was no one else in my class I really liked, and I jumped at the chance to meet someone new.

Elise and I didn't bond right away. She was loud and a little wild—the total opposite of me. So I showed her where to find the workbooks and how to use the wonky pencil sharpener, but I didn't think we would be real friends.

Then, on her third day at school, an alarm started blaring. Everyone thought it was a typical tornado drill until we looked outside and saw the dark clouds and trees blowing.

This wasn't a drill.

Elise and I crouched together under the same desk, doing the whole cover-your-head thing. I assumed she would talk and laugh like usual, but she was as terrified as me. While the other kids were making noise and complaining to the teacher, Elise and I clutched each other's shaking hands and cried.

When the tornado warning ended and we emerged from under the desk, some boy I don't remember laughed at my red face and watery eyes. Elise said—and I'll never forget her exact words—"having a red face is better than having a frog face." After that, we had no choice but to become friends.

Sitting with Elise on this bed might be the first time we've held each other since that terrifying afternoon in Ms. Matterson's third-grade class. Girls like Naomi and Adeline are always hugging each other, but my friends and I aren't like that. I'm not a touchy-feely person, mostly because you can never know if somebody is clean.

"Hello, Elise and Shannon?!" Mr. Bryant calls. "Are you two alive?"

"Huh?" I look around to see the entire cast standing in the wings, staring at me and Elise.

"Sorry, what?" Elise asks. We're still holding on to each other.

"We're starting at Gretl's entrance but with the new places. Did you hear anything I just said?"

"Sorry, sorry."

Elise and I scramble off the bed and join everyone else behind the heavy black curtains. I was too busy daydreaming to hear Mr. Bryant's instructions, but Elise rarely misses anything during rehearsal. One peek over my shoulder reveals that her face is bright pink. I bite my bottom lip. I don't want to get my hopes up, but part of me wonders if Elise was thinking about us hiding under that desk too.

After a full hour spent yodeling and skipping around the too-small bed, Naomi has to remind Mr. Bryant that rehearsal ended ten minutes ago. He stares at his watch in disbelief, shocked by the passage of time. I'm not at all surprised. My legs are exhausted from all the dancing, and my T-shirt and leggings are covered in sweat. I can't wait to get home and take a shower. Just thinking about stepping into the steaming water is comforting.

"I guess we have to end here." Mr. Bryant sounds frustrated. "Good work, people. That was almost decent by the end."

"High praise coming from him," Adeline whispers. "He's never happy at this point in rehearsals."

"Look, I want this experience to be fun, but everyone keep in mind that we have real competition this summer." Mr. Bryant's voice grows more animated, proving Adeline's point. "Another theater doing the same show is nothing short of disaster."

"Well, that's inspiring," Naomi says.

"I'm trying to motivate you." Mr. Bryant gestures wildly. "Is the situation unfortunate? Yes. Some of the actors downtown are pros. But we can work twice as hard and put on twice the show they do! I need focus. I need determination. And I need you to have your lines memorized by yesterday!"

"Ned, honey, I think that's enough." Mrs. Davis wanders onstage and places a hand on Mr. Bryant's shoulder. Did she call him Ned? And *honey*? Out of instinct, my eyes find Elise. She's staring back at me, her mouth hanging open. Is Adeline's mother dating Mr. Bryant? I didn't know either of them was single. I look to Adeline—if they're a couple, she must know—but she's staring at her phone.

"In addition to all that focus and determination, we also want to have fun, yes?" Mrs. Davis asks, to which Mr. Bryant shrugs. He's obviously more invested in outperforming Northern Rep than having a good time. "So in the spirit of fun, Adeline and I want to have everyone over to our house this Friday night. We're going to screen *The Sound of Music* movie, order some pizza, and have lots of fun! Right, Addy?"

"Uh-huh." Adeline doesn't look up from her phone.

"I've emailed your parents with the details," Mrs. Davis says. "We hope to see you there."

With that, everyone grabs their stuff and starts filing out of the auditorium into the sunlit lobby. Elise is out the door first, and I'm tempted to run after her. There were two real moments that made me hopeful for our friendship. But the last time I chased her, everything fell apart and I don't want to press my luck.

Still, I saw a glimpse of the old Elise and Shannon today. Of what we used to be. Of what we still could be, I hope. The party at Adeline's gives me the perfect opportunity. If I rehearse a compelling please-be-my-friend-again speech, wait for an opening during the movie, and pull Elise aside to make my case, maybe—just maybe—I can win her back.

A BOY ON A PORCH SWING

Fatima: Don't hate me.

Me: NOOOOOOO! DON'T SAY YOU CAN'T COME!!!!

I bounce my fist against my thighs as I wait for Fatima to respond. We worked out a foolproof plan last night. During one of the boring scenes, I'll ask Elise if we can talk in another room. Fatima will come with us, to be a referee if we need it. I'll calmly tell Elise how much I miss her and ask why she doesn't want to be friends with me. Ideally, we'll talk, maybe cry a bit, and then promise to never fight again. It's the perfect plan.

Fatima: Sorry. I've thrown up three times tonight. My mom thinks it's food poisoning.

It *was* the perfect plan. But now Fatima's not coming. Who knows if Elise will even talk to me without Fatima around? But I can't be annoyed with someone who's stuck at home vomiting.

Me: Wow that sucks. I hope you feel better soon!!!

Fatima: Thanks. Don't chicken out! You can do it!

From the moment I arrive at Adeline's house, I start second-guessing myself. I'm not sure how to get Elise alone because the house is packed. Between the big cast, all the techies, and a ton of parents, there are people everywhere. Elise is already surrounded by Adeline, Naomi, and a bunch of girls I barely know. Her new nun friends.

I grab a piece of pizza and find a spot on the floor next to Micah, who immediately starts chatting about his favorite movie musicals of all time. I nod along as he argues that *Singin' in the Rain* is the best ever, even if it's super old, but my eyes rarely leave Elise. Even when Mrs. Davis dims the lights and the television glows with a panoramic view of the Alps, I have one focus.

I consider approaching Elise at the beginning when Maria is still in the convent, but that seems too soon. And once our songs start, I'm singing along with everyone else. Through it all, though, I'm watching Elise. I know her better than anyone else in the room, and I know the perfect opportunity is coming.

We're reaching the end of the movie, and just as I hoped, Elise says something about going to the bathroom. She won't admit this to anyone but me and Fatima, but the scene where the kids are hiding from the soldiers terrifies her. When we watch the movie together, we always fast-forward through that part.

As Elise leaves the room, I jump up from my spot on the floor and weave through the sea of bodies, keeping her purple hair in sight. By the time I catch up with her, she's heading into the bathroom. It's not ideal, but it may be my only chance.

"Can we talk for a minute?" I ask. "Please?"

Elise whirls around to face me. Her eyes are narrowed, but she doesn't say no right away, so I launch into the speech I spent all day preparing. "I miss you a lot. The way you've been treating me really hurts my feelings. But the worst part is not knowing what I did wrong. I want to apologize, but I don't understand what's happening."

As I reach the end of my monologue, Elise's face relaxes. It's the same, familiar glimpse of my friend I saw at rehearsal yesterday, which makes me hopeful. Elise leans against the bathroom doorway and studies me, like she's trying to choose the right words. I wait patiently. I will stand here all night if it means Elise talking to me again.

"I wasn't trying to be mean," Elise says finally. "I just needed a little break from hanging out."

"But why?!" I'm way too loud.

"Shhh!" Elise pulls me all the way into the bathroom and shuts the door. She perches on the closed toilet seat, her body hunched over. Normally, Elise towers above me with her long torso and slender legs, but in here, she looks small.

"Look, I wasn't happy when you auditioned for the musical, okay?" She picks at her nail. "It was hard for me to deal with."

"But you said it was okay." Technically, that's true. But if I'm being honest, I always knew Elise wasn't one hundred percent cool with me getting onstage. Maybe not even fifty percent. But it wasn't her decision to make. And she *said* she didn't mind.

"Yeah, I know." Elise shrugs. "I guess I didn't expect you to be, like, really good? But you were and it made me uncomfortable."

"Seriously?" I try to keep my voice level. "You wanted me to fail. Is that right? You wanted my audition to be terrible?" I don't know what I expected Elise to say, but certainly not this. I knew she was disappointed with her performance, but her being angry at my success feels different.

"No, not *terrible*." Elise sighs. "I just didn't think you would be so amazing. And you didn't even practice or anything. It didn't seem fair."

"We both tried out and we both got cast," I say. The words are coming faster than my brain can think. "We're both von Trapp kids. How is that not fair? Are you jealous or something?"

It's only when I shout the word at Elise that I realize it's one hundred percent true. My best friend is jealous of me. She's jealous that I'm a decent singer. She's jealous that Mr. Bryant saw something in me.

"I'm not *jealous*." Elise is horrified by my accusation. "I think it's sweet Mr. Bryant gave you a chance. It was nice of him to give you Brigitta."

"NICE? SWEET?!" My fists are clenched at my side and I'm full-on screaming. I can see my scrunched-up face in the mirror and I look like a monster. I don't think I've ever been this angry before. I didn't realize I *could* be this angry. "Don't act like I'm some charity case when we both know Brigitta is the better part. *Brigitta* has all the good lines. *Brigitta* has the one-on-one scene with Maria. If your audition hadn't sucked so much, that would have been you. But it did suck, and now you're so jealous of me you can barely *speak* to me."

Elise looks like I slapped her. Her eyes are full of tears and her entire body is trembling. Half of me feels guilty, but the other half is still seething. I don't know which half to trust, so I turn around and run out of the room, leaving Elise slumped over on the toilet seat.

I keep running, past the curious looks of people who probably heard us shouting, through the open front door and into the night. I collapse on a wooden porch swing and cry.

I don't fully remember everything I yelled at Elise, but I'm confident our friendship is officially over. She was mad at me before I said those terrible things. Now she's going to be livid. I know I should apologize, but I can't stop thinking about what she's put me through. She's been ignoring me and excluding me. She's been acting like I don't exist at all. All because she's jealous. I deserve an apology from her too.

"I thought I saw you come outside." I look up to see someone hovering by the door. The dark silhouette turns into Micah as he walks toward me. "Can I join you?" He gestures to the porch swing.

"Sure." I scoot over and wipe the stray tears from my cheeks. Even if you ignore the sniffling, it's still obvious I've been crying. Nobody leaves a party to sit on the front porch unless something's wrong.

"You didn't want to stay for the end of the movie?" I ask.

"Nah." Micah sits down next to me, then uses his feet to rock us back and forth. The wooden swing creaks loudly.

"I know how it turns out. And there's nobody worth talking to inside."

"Oh. Yeah." I'm not sure what that implies. If I'm the only person outside, does that mean Micah only wants to hang out with me? Normally, I would immediately text my friends and ask their opinion. Except one friend is home vomiting and the other friend will likely never speak to me again.

"I think it's cool what you're doing," Micah says.

"Huh?" I ask, then grimace at my not-so-intelligent response. "It's cool that I'm sitting alone on a porch swing because I broke up with my best friend?" I sigh. "Sorry. It's been a bad night."

"No, I meant it's cool that . . . never mind." Micah doesn't say anything more. I peer at him through the darkness, but I can't see his expression.

"You can tell me," I say.

"Okay." Micah takes a deep breath, and I'm suddenly afraid he's about to profess his love for me on this very porch swing. I have no clue how I would respond. Is there a protocol for this sort of thing?

"You know I have an older sister?" he asks finally.

"Yeah?" That is totally not what I was expecting.

"She has anxiety. And OCD. And depression." I freeze as Micah lists off words that are way too familiar to me. He talks about mental illness like he's describing the lunch menu. And why is he saying these things to me?

"Yeah?" I say again. I don't want to give anything away.

"The OCD is especially hard on her. She's been in therapy her whole life."

"So your sister . . . Oh." Suddenly, everything makes sense. Micah wasn't in the waiting room for his own session. He was waiting for his sister.

"Her big thing is locks," Micah says. "Mary checks every lock in our house a bunch of times before she goes to bed." I think he's staring at me, but I can't tell for sure. "When she was younger, she was scared of being kidnapped, and it turned into an obsession. I don't think she's afraid anymore, but she still checks the locks."

I fiddle with the hem of my shirt. Micah reaches out and brushes his fingers against my forearm. My entire body tenses, and he jerks his hand away. Nobody besides Ariel has ever really *gotten* what my OCD feels like. But, somehow, the boy sitting next to me on the porch swing is saying all the right things.

"How did you know?" I ask eventually, my voice barely above a whisper.

He leans closer and lowers his voice. "That you have OCD?"

"Yeah. Did you see . . . ? Just . . . how did you know?"

"I know what it looks like," Micah says. "With my sister . . . it's a big part of my life."

"You just knew?"

"Yeah. Sorry. After I saw you in the waiting room, I was a little curious." His voice sounds guilty to admit this, but I understand completely. I've been wondering what's wrong with him from the moment I saw him at Ariel's office too. "With the ChapStick and the hand washing . . . I figured it out."

I don't respond.

"It's not a bad thing, though," Micah adds quickly. "And I didn't want to make you uncomfortable. I guess I meant . . . if you ever need a friend who gets it"—Micah nudges his shoulder against mine—"I'm around."

"Thanks." I'm glad for the darkness because I'm positive my face is the color of a cherry tomato.

Together, Micah and I swing in silence. With Elise and Fatima, there's rarely a quiet moment. Somebody always has something to say. But with Micah, the silence isn't awkward or weird. It's just peaceful. I can hear bursts of laughter and shouting inside, but it's easy to ignore the commotion out here. At least until the door flies open and a hysterical Adeline runs onto the porch. Micah and I stop swinging and our bodies tense in unison.

"I thought he would say yes!" Adeline is crying into her cell phone. "No, I'm going for a drive. My house is full of people." She slams the door behind her and turns to walk down the steps. That's when she sees me and Micah.

"You're friends with Fatima, right?" Adeline points an accusatory finger at me.

"Yes?" I slouch down on the porch swing. I can't handle another person being angry with me.

"Well, you tell Fatima to tell her brother that he sucks!" She emits a sound that's half hiccup, half sob.

I would normally tell Adeline to share that information with Amir herself, but arguing with a distraught teenager probably isn't smart. So I nod—not that Adeline can see me—and watch as she runs across the front lawn.

When her car door slams shut, Micah and I both explode with laughter. We're not laughing *at* Adeline— I'm assuming Amir refused to go out with her, which is terrible—but at the ridiculousness of the situation. Between me and Elise shouting in the bathroom and the host running away in tears, this night is truly a disaster. I'm not sure Mrs. Davis will be eager to host any more parties at her house.

I don't know if it's the dark cover of night or the warm feeling fluttering in my chest, but something makes me bold. I slide my hand across the weathered wood until I feel the warmth of Micah's palm. I timidly rest my hand on his, and he squeezes enthusiastically—*too* enthusiastically— in return.

"Ow!" I pull my hand away, hoping he didn't crush anything. Who knew a twelve-year-old could have such a powerful grip?

"Oh no. I'm so sorry." Micah buries his face in his hands, then cocks his head to look back up at me like a puppy who misbehaved. "I literally hurt you. Wow. *Great job, Micah,*" he scolds himself.

"No, it's okay!" I'm unable to contain my laughter. "Remember when Robert stepped on my hand during rehearsal? That hurt a lot worse."

I reach for his hand again, boldly this time. I don't shake hands—I don't even high-five my friends—but something about holding Micah's hand feels different. I'm not panicking about needing to find a sink. I just feel happy.

This time, Micah holds my hand gently, like I'm a human being with bones and nerves rather than a stress ball. "Is this okay?" he asks.

"Yes!" I answer before he's even finished asking the question.

Way better than okay, I think.

The world may be falling to pieces all around me, but this moment is perfect. I'm with a boy on a porch swing. He's holding my hand. And though I can't see him in the darkness, I get the feeling he's smiling as wide as me.

SCRABBLE, CRIBBAGE, AND OTHER OLD-PERSON GAMES

"MOM!" I holler from my bedroom. "I can't find my ChapStick!"

I just woke up, and my ChapStick isn't in its usual spot. I forgot to leave a tube under my pillow before falling asleep, and now my lips are unbearably dry.

"I can't hear you!" Mom yells back.

I switch from slippers to Vans and run down the stairs. Grandma Ruby is sitting in her usual spot at the dining table with a cup of coffee and a blueberry scone. Mom is standing in the kitchen, rummaging through her purse. She pulls out her sunglasses and then her keys.

"Where are you going? And why are you leaving so early?" I ask Mom.

"It's ten-thirty," Grandma Ruby says dryly. "The rest of the household has been awake for several hours, Shannon."

"Right." I'm not normally a late sleeper, especially with Grandma Ruby staying in my bedroom, but I didn't fall asleep until two in the morning. After I got home from the movie screening, I spent an hour texting with Fatima, another hour dissecting every detail of the night with Mom, and then three hours alternating between crying about Elise and fantasizing about Micah holding my hand again. It's no wonder I didn't wake up to Grandma Ruby stomping around my room.

"Sorry, sweetie. I have a ton of errands to run," Mom says. "Are you feeling any better this morning?"

"A little, I guess." I didn't wake up crying, so that's progress. "Except I can't find any ChapStick."

"Did you look in your bathroom drawers?"

"Yup."

"Your backpack?"

"Yup."

"Bedside table?"

"Yeah, I checked all the normal spots."

Because I can't live without ChapStick, Mom keeps a billion spare tubes around our house. In her bedroom, in the laundry room, in sock drawers and linen cabinets. The problem, of course, is that I raid those hiding spots whenever I'm running low. Which inevitably causes me to panic because I can't find ChapStick when I need it most.

"Oh, I have hiding spots you don't know about." Mom

crosses the kitchen to the spice rack and starts shaking glass jars and plastic containers. I watch her in confusion. "But seriously, sweetie. You have to tell me before you run out completely." She pops open a container of Cajun seasoning and out falls the familiar blue and white tube.

"Thank you, thank you, thank you!"

Mom tosses the ChapStick to me and grabs her purse. "I'll be back later," she says. "Have a good day with your grandmother, okay?"

I nod and wave goodbye, though having a good day seems unlikely. There's no rehearsal on Saturday, Fatima is still feeling sick, and I made things a thousand times worse with Elise. The only person besides Grandma Ruby I might be able to talk to is Micah, and I don't have his number. Well, I could probably find his number in the theater directory. But texting him randomly feels bold, and I'm less confident in the light of day.

Grandma Ruby watches as I peel the plastic wrapper off the fresh tube of ChapStick and coat my lips three times. When I snap the cap back on, she snatches it from my hands.

"Hey, I need that!"

"Do you need the ChapStick or does your brain *think* you need the ChapStick?"

"Isn't that the same thing?" I'm really not in the mood for a philosophical debate this early in the morning. Or not so early in the morning, as Grandma Ruby would correct me.

"Didn't I overhear you telling your mother something about going fifteen minutes without using ChapStick?"

"Um . . ." I stare at my feet. I may have lied to Ariel again this week at therapy. When I told her I walked across my whole bedroom in the wrong shoes—which I could totally do if I tried—she congratulated me and came up with a new challenge. Whenever I have the urge to put on ChapStick, I'm supposed to wait fifteen minutes and see if I still need to. It sounds simple enough, but I've kinda been occupied with my entire life falling apart. I lick my lips. I know rationally that only makes them dryer, but it's all I can think about.

"Yeah, but that's for next week," I say. "I don't need to do the ChapStick thing right now."

"Nonsense," Grandma Ruby says. "You don't have any other plans today." With that, she opens the refrigerator door, tosses my ChapStick inside, and places her hands on her hips.

"But I need—"

"What you need is something else to occupy that overactive brain of yours for fifteen minutes." Grandma Ruby takes me by the shoulders and propels me into the dining room. "Come on. We're playing Scrabble."

Fourteen and a half minutes later, we've set up the game board and chosen seven random letter tiles from the cloth bag. Grandma Ruby is busy searching for her first word while I stare longingly at the fridge. I imagine my Chap-Stick inside, chilling next to the bell peppers and cucumbers. I lick my lips again and look at the clock.

"It's been fifteen minutes." I start to push myself up.

"Wait," Grandma Ruby says.

I glare at her. "Fifteen minutes. I completed the assignment."

"Can you go longer?" she asks.

"Well, maybe. But I don't need to because—"

"Excellent. Sit back down." Grandma Ruby turns back to the Scrabble board, spreading six letters across the center to spell F-R-I-G-I-D. "Are you keeping score?" she asks. "There's a double letter and a double word. That makes thirty points total."

"Okay, I got it." I write thirty on the legal pad Grandma Ruby found in the kitchen. "You know, this would be quicker if I could focus. And I would focus if my lips weren't so dry."

"Try fifteen more minutes," Grandma Ruby says, lighting a cigarette. Mom wouldn't want her smoking in the house, but I don't have the authority to enforce that rule. Instead, I stare at my tiles—a useless combination of vowels.

"Grandma, this is hard. My letters suck."

"There are no bad Scrabble tiles, only bad Scrabble players."

"So you're calling me a bad Scrabble player?"

Grandma Ruby chooses not to respond, but the answer is obvious. A few turns later and she's totally crushing me. She clearly doesn't believe in going easy on your grandchildren. The score is 123 to 35, and her turns keep getting better. I plop down an E and an A to make the word T-E-A. Three whole points for me.

"Really, Shannon? That's the best you can do?"

"I only have vowels," I say. Which is pretty much true. I also have an X and a J, but those are impossible to use.

"Nope." Grandma Ruby pushes the tiles back toward me. "Find something better."

I sigh dramatically and look for a better word. Eventually, I come up with E-X-E-S. It's not a 50 pointer, but Grandma nods in approval. I check my phone. It's now been thirty minutes since I promised I would try another fifteen.

"Hey, it's way past time," I say.

"Well, do you *need* ChapStick?" Grandma Ruby doesn't look up from her letters.

"Well . . ." Now that I'm thinking about my lips, they feel dry. But it's not the worst thing I've ever experienced. And focusing on the game is a decent distraction. "I guess I could go a little longer if—"

"Good. That's eighteen points for me." Grandma Ruby arranges her letters to spell APPLE. "Your turn."

And so the day continues. After we conclude our Scrabble game, Grandma teaches me gin rummy. When I proclaim that rummy is boring, we switch to cribbage. Unlike the noisy games of Go Fish I used to play with Mom, Grandma Ruby believes chatting while playing is an unnecessary distraction. Other than her explanation of the rules and frequent complaints when I take too long, the house is silent. It's the most relaxed I've felt in a long time. It may be an old person game, but I'm actually good at cribbage. And it's nice to focus on something that isn't my own life.

When Mom walks through the door, arms weighed down with bags of groceries, I'm surprised to see her. One look at the kitchen clock, and I'm even more surprised. It's already 1:30. I was so engrossed in our game that I didn't realize we missed lunch.

"Well . . . this seems fun." Mom glances back and forth between me, Grandma Ruby, and the cards strewn across the cribbage board on our table. "Did you have a good morning, Shannon?"

"Yeah, we had so much fun!" I ditch our game and follow Mom into the kitchen. Grandma Ruby grunts, frustrated by the interruption, but follows me anyway. "We played Scrabble and gin rummy and cribbage. I think I liked cribbage the best." I help Mom put away the groceries as I tell her all about my cribbage triumphs. Grandma Ruby clucks her tongue. She is not a gracious loser.

"That's wonderful, sweetie," Mom says. "It's great to see you so relaxed." She pauses as she pulls a head of cabbage from a paper bag. "Maybe you should be spending more time at home. I'm worried the stress of the play is making your OCD worse."

"MOM!" She still doesn't trust that I'm capable of acting in a musical, and it's so frustrating.

"Sorry, sorry. I know you're fine." Mom holds up her hands and I smile. She tosses the cabbage into the refrigerator while I shove Cheez-Its and OREOs into the cupboard. Grandma Ruby makes no effort to help.

"Uh, Shannon?" Mom asks.

"Yeah?"

"Why is your ChapStick in the fridge?" I turn around, and Mom hands me the chilled tube. I hadn't thought about my lips in hours, but I'm suddenly overwhelmed by how dry they are. I pop off the cap and lather layer after layer on my lips.

"Grandma Ruby put my ChapStick in the refrigerator," I say after I've applied nine coats. I needed three sets of three to make up for an entire morning with chapped lips.

"Why on earth would you put her ChapStick in the refrigerator?!" Mom's eyes widen, and she crosses her arms.

"She was obsessing," Grandma says. I look down in embarrassment. I know Grandma Ruby doesn't understand my OCD like Mom and Ariel, but she didn't seem to be judging me today like she usually does.

"So . . . so what?" Mom sputters as she angrily shoves more vegetables into the fridge. "Are you a licensed psychiatrist? Do you have a medical degree? Who are you to decide what Shannon needs?"

"Oh hush," Grandma Ruby says. "It was her therapist's idea. And she barely noticed it was missing. Isn't that right, Shannon?"

"Um . . ." I am pretty impressed with myself. I don't remember the last time I went so long without using Chap-Stick. Now I can honestly tell Ariel I completed one of her silly assignments. I don't say any of that out loud, though. "I guess . . . I don't know."

In the seconds before Mom and Grandma Ruby start fighting again, I make my escape. I run upstairs, switch shoes, and lock my bedroom door. All I want is to regain some of the focus I had while playing games, but it's too late. I can't stop thinking about Elise and Fatima and

Mom and Ariel and Micah and the musical and the arguing and my ChapStick and my shoes. My brain may have been distracted for a little while, but it's like the OCD switched right back on and then went into overdrive. I'm panting and scrubbing my fingernails with soap when my phone rings.

I dry my hands before answering. It's a Minnesota number I don't recognize, and my chest seizes with hope. "Hello?" I breathe into the phone.

"Hey, uh, is this Shannon?"

I grin as Micah's timid voice reaches my ear and I can feel my worries recede. So what if Elise doesn't want to apologize? A boy just called me. Not only that, but he also searched the theater directory, and *then* called me. That's dedication.

"Hey, Micah! Yeah, this is Shannon." I'm still breathing a bit heavily from my frantic hand washing.

"Are you okay? You sound like you're running a marathon or something."

"Um, definitely not. I can barely handle the dance steps in 'Do-Re-Mi.'"

Micah laughs, which was my goal. I love hearing him laugh. The warm crackle of his voice makes me blush.

"So . . . ," he says. "I don't remember if I told you, but my dad runs a food truck."

"Really? No way!" Before Grandma Ruby moved in,

Mom and I watched lots of Food Network, and we loved any show with food trucks.

"Yeah, it's called Sam's Skewers. Basically any kind of food on a stick. It . . . it's not as weird as it sounds," Micah stammers, like this is somehow embarrassing, but I think his dad's job sounds incredible. "Anyway, there's a food truck festival happening downtown tomorrow, and I was wondering if you wanted to go."

"Really?" my voice squeaks out.

"If you don't want—" Micah starts to take back his offer before I've even answered. I can feel his nervousness radiating through the phone.

"No, no!" I cut him off, hopefully in a reassuring way. "I would love to go." I glance at the paper calendar on my desk. "I'm rehearsing my scene with Maria tomorrow morning, but maybe after that?"

"Oh." Micah's voice falls. "I have to be there all day. I help my dad set up."

"That's okay." I want to make Micah sound happy again. And I *really* want to eat his dad's skewers. "What if I meet you there? I can get a ride from my mom if you text me the address."

"Seriously? That's awesome. I'll send you the info."

"Perfect," I say. And then the next sentence leaves my mouth before I can overthink it. "It's a date."

Micah doesn't protest.

MAGIC

The theater is empty when I arrive for my private rehearsal with Naomi. Spooky empty.

No parents waiting in the hallway, subtly bragging about their kids. No techies dragging plywood into the set shop or showing off the costume pieces they found at Goodwill. No actors warming up or running lines. Just me alone in the empty atrium with my purse and script in hand.

I smooth my dress and head for the heavy oak doors that lead into the auditorium. I insisted my outing with Micah wasn't a date—it's just two friends eating skewers, I'd argued—but Mom and I both knew better. She wanted me to wear something nice to mark the occasion, so I settled on a navy-blue T-shirt dress. It's casual enough for an outdoor event featuring BBQ sauce and fried pickles, but slightly cuter than my normal ensemble of jean shorts and a faded gymnastics shirt.

The door creaks as I push it open, but I don't step inside. The theater is pitch-black, which means Mr. Bryant must not have arrived yet. If Fatima were here, she could turn on the lights from the booth, but I don't have that skill. I hover in the doorway, spreading ChapStick across my lips, unsure of where to go next.

"Who's there?" a voice calls from the stage.

"It's Shannon!" I yell back. "Is that you, Naomi?" I'm fairly certain I recognize the older girl's voice, but the darkness is confusing my senses.

"Yup!" A flashlight flips on, illuminating Naomi's face from below.

"What in the world?!" I jump back, banging my elbow against the door. The warm glow of the flashlight shines across her dark brown skin, turning her a terrifying shade of orange. She looks like a character from a horror movie or an actor in a haunted house. "That's scary."

"Sorry!" She laughs, pulling the flashlight away from her face. It's still creepy in here, but at least Naomi looks human again. "Come join me. Mr. Bryant texted and said he's running late."

I walk down the aisle, timidly at first, but then I realize I have a flashlight too. I grab my phone and maximize the brightness. Mr. Bryant isn't here, so I ignore his stairs-only rule and launch myself belly-first onto the stage like the older kids. I don't have the practice, though, so I end up dropping my phone and possibly bruising a few ribs. I'm out of breath and slightly embarrassed when I crawl next to Naomi, but I don't need to worry. The older girl is lying flat on her back, staring upward.

"Lie down." Naomi pats the stage next to her.

"Okay." I slide onto my back, making sure my palms don't touch the ground. I don't want to start my special rehearsal with a long trip to the bathroom.

"Isn't it pretty?" Naomi asks.

"Um . . ." If the stage lights were on, we would be staring at jumbo lightbulbs and wiring, but there's only darkness above us now. I squint at the emptiness, trying to picture the beauty Naomi sees. I guess the absence of something can also be beautiful. Like when my OCD is at a minimum, and I almost forget it's there.

"Yeah, I see what you mean," I say. "It kinda looks like the night sky without the stars."

"Exactly." Naomi exhales. "I think I want to major in astronomy. Stars are so magical, you know?"

"Yeah," I say. And suddenly, my mind turns to a different kind of magic.

I used to think Mr. Bryant was corny when he talked about the magic of the theater. When I did gymnastics back in elementary school, my coaches never talked about the balance beam like it contained superpowers. But lying here with Naomi, I feel a bit of magic bubbling inside me.

Not literally, of course. I can't cast spells or turn Elise into a frog. But there's a magnetism in this auditorium even when nobody else is around. The heavy velvet curtains, the rows of metal lights, the musty smell of sawdust and stale popcorn—that special feeling is there whether you're in the costume closet or the set shop or the sound booth.

What I didn't know before a few weeks ago was how the magic ramps up when you become part of the cast. I like transforming into a different person when I'm on the stage, as if I truly can be anybody I want. I like being part of something that matters to so many people. And— even if I can only admit this in the total darkness of the theater—I like knowing there's something unbreakable connecting me and Elise, even when we're both running as fast as we can in opposite directions.

Mr. Bryant arrives fifteen minutes later, full of breathless apologies. He fumbles around in the booth for a moment before the stage lights turn on, blinding me out of my relaxed stupor.

"Sorry, sorry, sorry! I was stuck at the bank and then a

parent called me." Mr. Bryant bustles down the aisle with his usual leather messenger bag slung across his chest and a cardboard holder full of Starbucks drinks. "But I brought coffee. An iced latte for you . . ." He hands a cup to Naomi. "And, Shannon, I didn't know what you would like. So I got one of those pink drinks. That's a tween thing, right?" He hands me a venti-sized cup full of ice and pastel pink liquid. It both looks and smells slightly like Pepto-Bismol, but I take a sip and decide it's not so bad.

"Thank you so much," I say. Mr. Bryant waves his hand like it's nothing, and I wonder if this is how all his private rehearsals go. No wonder Elise was desperate to get the part of Brigitta.

"Okay, let's chat."

We only have two hours—well, an hour and forty-five minutes, now—so I was expecting to start blocking right away. But Mr. Bryant sits on the floor between me and Naomi and flips his script to the correct page.

"This scene is only a couple minutes long and there isn't any music, so some directors miss its importance." Mr. Bryant makes a face that implies those directors are very, very wrong. "However, I believe this exchange between Brigitta and Maria *defines* the end of Act I."

I flush with pride at the thought of being so integral to the play.

Mr. Bryant continues. "Though most people wouldn't

define the story in such simple terms, *The Sound of Music* is indeed a love story, correct?" Both Naomi and I nod. "But much of that is experienced through the innocence of the children. So in this scene, I want to feel your passion"—he points at Naomi—"and your snarky innocence." He looks to me.

I nod in agreement. That's a good way to describe Brigitta. She's funny and sassy, but I think deep down she feels insecure and timid about her place in the world. And when she reveals Captain von Trapp's true feelings to Maria, it's not her being silly. She loves Maria and clearly knows what she's doing.

"All right." He claps his hands. "On your feet. Let's start with both of you downstage right, in front of the stairs. We'll try it once through and see what happens naturally."

Naomi and I move into place; then Mr. Bryant cues us with the final line of the previous scene. After my practice session with Fatima, I feel super confident in my lines, so I focus on the emotion. I begin matter-of-factly, like I might tell my governess any other story. But when I reach the big reveal, when I tell Maria my father loves her, I let my voice fill with longing. If it were up to Brigitta, she would have her father marry Maria right this instant. Naomi matches my energy, and I'm feeling good about our performance when Mr. Bryant motions for us to stop. I think we kinda nailed it. But our director is leaning against the stage, his chin resting on his fists, looking not at all pleased.

"What's wrong?" Naomi shields her eyes from the stage lights.

"Well, the emotion was great. Especially you, Shannon." I feel giddy with pride, once again. "I'd like for both of you to slow down a bit, as usual. Don't rush the scene." Mr. Bryant vaults onto the stage—the exact way he instructs all of us *not* to—and sits cross-legged in front of us. "Neither of you moved that entire scene. I know I didn't give you specific blocking, but I want you moving around. Try again."

We run the scene a second time. I focus on slowing down my lines and extending the silent moments, mostly because I have no idea where to walk. Naomi wanders across the stage at one point, but it feels unnatural. Mr. Bryant cuts us off before the scene is finished.

"Okay, let's try this." He stands up and starts moving us around by the shoulders. This is more what I envisioned. I like being told exactly where to stand and when to move. "All right. We have Maria stage left and Brigitta stage right. At first, you're speaking from a distance. But as the moment gets more personal, I want you to move toward each other until you're both center stage. Got it?"

"I guess," Naomi says, her voice hesitant. I share her concern. I don't feel like Brigitta would start talking to Maria from across the room, but I can't exactly complain.

When Mr. Bryant told us to freestyle, my feet turned into concrete.

As I expected, this run is a major flop. Then Mr. Bryant has me standing center stage while Naomi paces nervously around me. It's an improvement, but not amazing. A few ideas later, and I'm sitting on the edge of the stage, my legs dangling into the audience while Naomi kneels behind me. It's kinda ridiculous, but I see what Mr. Bryant is going for.

"I like the levels," he rants, pacing back and forth. "But it's not right. And this scene needs to be perfect. You two are amazing, don't get me wrong. The problem is here." He points two thumbs at himself. Mr. Bryant wasn't kidding about taking this scene seriously. I've never seen him this troubled at a rehearsal, not even when Riya fell offstage and Mrs. Davis thought she might have a concussion.

"Do you two have any brilliant ideas you're holding back?" Our director looks between me and Naomi, desperate for inspiration. We've run five minutes over time, and the scene still isn't finished. "Seriously, there are no bad ideas here. Except for mine. Those are bad ideas."

"Are you telling me those stairs are just for decoration?" A raspy voice emerges from the back of the auditorium. A lump grows in my throat as Grandma Ruby ambles down the aisle like she owns the place. I gesture wildly, motioning for her to return to the car. Mr. Bryant has a strict "no parents" policy, and I'm certain that extends to grand-parents too. But my stubborn grandmother ignores my flailing and stares straight at Mr. Bryant.

"If you want levels, place Brigitta on the grand stair-case. This is the scene after she's spying on the party guests, correct?"

"I . . . uh . . . don't know who you are"—Mr. Bryant runs one hand across his face—"but that is brilliant," he con-cedes. "I should have had Brigitta on the stairs from the beginning. Much more intimate."

"Do you know her?" Naomi whispers.

"Yeah." Embarrassment runs through me like a hot cur-rent. Grandma Ruby must have insisted on accompanying Mom in the car, probably to wish me luck on my not-a-date with Micah. But why Mom allowed her to wander into the auditorium without supervision is a mystery.

"Grandma Ruby," I say, clearing my throat, "these are closed rehearsals." It's something I've heard Mr. Bryant say to other misguided parents.

"This is your grandma, Shannon?" Mr. Bryant turns to me, but he sounds relieved, not angry. I suppose a grand-mother bursting into rehearsal is better than a serial killer.

"Yes," Grandma Ruby answers for me, extending her hand to the much younger man. "Ruby Carter, former re-gional theater actress."

I groan internally.

"Well, Mrs. Carter—"

"It's *Ms.* Carter," Grandma Ruby corrects him, just like I feared she would. "I've never had a man, and I don't plan on changing that now. You get to be my age and they simply become unnecessary." She makes a shooing motion with her hand, and Mr. Bryant grins even wider.

"Well, Ms. Carter. We're running out of time, but let's get Shannon on the staircase to see if your idea works."

Without making eye contact with Grandma Ruby, I climb halfway up the fake marble stairs and sit with my knees tucked to my chest. Naomi begins downstage, then crosses upstage when she sees me huddled on the staircase. We sit together for half the dialogue, and it feels more loving, exactly like Mr. Bryant wanted.

Then, on my big line, I stand up and tell Maria with conviction that my father loves her. It's not quite how I performed the line before, but it feels right.

Both Mr. Bryant and Grandma Ruby are clapping when the scene ends. That was a thousand times better than our first attempt. This version is full of emotion and energy, like Maria and Brigitta were truly alive on the stage. Naomi wraps one arm around my shoulders and squeezes. Then she leans down and whispers into my ear, "You were amazing, Shannon."

I'm buzzing too much to respond. As I gather my things and follow Grandma Ruby out of the auditorium,

I stop multiple times to stare behind me. I'm finding it difficult to leave even though rehearsal is over. It's like an invisible force pulls me back to the stage. Something like a rope or a magnet or . . . I think back to the beginning of rehearsal when Naomi and I were on our backs staring at the pretend stars . . . something like magic.

SAM'S SKEWERS

The drive downtown is painfully awkward.

Grandma Ruby insisted on tagging along, which would be nice if she and Mom were speaking to each other. But their argument about my ChapStick turned into a fight about a million other things. Mom not finishing graduate school. Mom coddling me too much. Mom not making enough money. And this isn't like most fights when they're shouting one minute and joking the next. This fight feels permanent.

As we get closer to our destination, my excitement about the food truck festival turns into uncertainty. If this is a date, does that mean Micah wants to be my boyfriend? How can I possibly ask that question without melting into a puddle of embarrassment? And what would having a boyfriend even mean? Holding hands at rehearsal?

Texting each other good night? I tug at the hem of my T-shirt dress. Maybe I should have worn something more casual.

"Must we run the air conditioner constantly?" Grandma Ruby asks.

"It's ninety degrees outside, so yes," Mom snaps.

I've enjoyed having Grandma Ruby around more than I anticipated, but I desperately wish she wasn't in the passenger seat right now. If it were just me and Mom, we could dissect every text between me and Micah and prepare emergency conversation starters. But if I tell Grandma Ruby I'm nervous about this date, she'll recount some story about a boy she took to the movies when she was my age. If they even had movies back then.

There are cars lining the streets around the festival, and all the parking garages cost money. Mom circles a few times, looking for an empty space, but nothing appears. Grandma Ruby's eyes narrow, and I imagine her launching into a speech about wasting gas or overcrowding city streets.

"You can drop me off," I say. "I know where to meet Micah."

"Are you sure?" Mom asks, but she's already pulling into a fire lane. "Text me if you need anything. You can get a ride home with Micah's father?"

"Yup. I'm good." I smooth my dress once more, apply three layers of ChapStick, and climb out of the car. "Thanks for the ride," I say. "And thanks for coming, Grandma," I add when I see her lips purse.

The food truck festival is even grander than I imagined. Big, rectangular trucks in every color of the rainbow fill an entire city block. People of all ages roam the square, balancing plates of food, ice cream cones, and to-go cups. Dogs race in circles around their owners, pulling on leashes and snatching bits of fallen food.

As I walk farther into the park, my senses are over-whelmed by a hundred different aromas—the unmistakable spices of curry chicken, the bitterness of freshly brewed coffee, the enticing odor of deep-fried everything. My stomach grumbles.

"Shannon, hey!"

I grin when I see Micah jumping up and down next to a neon-orange truck. He's wearing khaki cargo shorts, a plain red T-shirt, and a white apron tied around his waist. I feel overdressed next to him, but I also wasn't working in a metal box all morning.

"Hey! Is this your dad's truck?" I jog the last few steps to meet Micah.

He leans forward like he wants to hug me, but I side-step his embrace to admire the food truck. I feel a twinge of guilt—it's not that I don't want to hug Micah. I just don't hug anybody who's covered in that much sweat. Just looking at his damp T-shirt makes me feel twitchy.

"Yup. Sam's Skewers." Micah doesn't seem to register my snub. He presents the food truck with an arm flourish. There are probably ten people in line, which is way more than any of the neighboring trucks. Nobody seems at all interested in the sashimi truck next door. Minnesota isn't known for its high-quality sushi.

"This is so cool." I study the menu. There are six options, all of them "on a stick." I like the simplicity. Sometimes when I go to fancy restaurants with Mom, I get over-whelmed by all the choices. But this is straightforward. *Chicken and Waffles on a Stick. Fruit Salad on a Stick. Steak Fajitas on a Stick.*

"You hungry?" Micah asks.

"Definitely. I barely ate before rehearsal."

"Okay, I'll hook you up."

I was planning to wait in line and pay for my food like a normal customer, but Micah skirts past the crowd and disappears into the truck. When he appears two minutes later, he's swapped the apron for a baseball cap. He hands me a plate with two different skewers.

"Dad's chicken and waffles are the best. And then I got you cheesecake on a stick." Micah shrugs. "We had extra."

"This is perfect." I take a bite of the chicken and waffle

skewer, being sure to get some of each. Micah is watching me carefully, but I don't have to fake a reaction. The spiciness of the batter contrasts perfectly with the sweet and sticky waffle. I moan in approval, wiping away the syrup dripping down my chin. Micah's whole face lights up as I take another giant bite.

"This is seriously so good," I mumble through a mouthful of food. Manners don't seem to be a top priority at the food truck festival. "Do you eat this every single day?"

"When my dad first opened the truck, then yeah, basically. It gets boring after a while." Micah leads me to the truck with the longest line in the whole park. "This one is my favorite," he says. "Don't tell my dad."

The pink and yellow truck—called "Lotta Tots"—features a menu full of tater tots: chili tots, nacho tots, pizza tots. I'm not at all surprised this place is popular. While Minnesota isn't known for its raw fish, tater tots are our specialty.

I continue munching on my skewers while we wait in line. Micah hums and kicks a pebble between his feet. We're surrounded by people talking and laughing, but the silence between us suddenly feels daunting. I should have brainstormed conversation topics with Mom. I try not to blame Grandma Ruby for butting into our time.

"So how was your private rehearsal?" Micah asks after a minute, and I exhale in relief.

I catch him up on all the details, including my grand-mother's surprise appearance at the end. Sometimes when I'm talking to friends—even Elise and Fatima—I feel like they're not really listening. Like they're just waiting until it's their turn to talk. But Micah hangs on every word I say. It makes me feel special.

"I can't wait to see the scene." Micah pauses to place his order for tater tot nachos and a Sprite.

"Yeah, it was fun to focus on my acting. I've been a little distracted during rehearsals. You know . . . with the whole Elise thing." I shove the cheesecake skewer into my mouth before I spew more unnecessary information. Micah doesn't care about the drama between me and my friends. And what if he thinks I'm one of those girls who gossips constantly? I would hate that.

After his number is called and Micah grabs his totchos, we head toward an empty park bench. The familiarity of the weathered wood is comforting. A couple nights ago, when Micah and I sat on the porch swing together, our conversation was easy. I don't need to obsess over every word I say with him.

"I did notice you were hanging out with her less. Not that I mind, of course." Micah winks and offers me a tater tot. I would cringe if anybody but him said that, but I find myself blushing instead.

"Yeah." I chew on the tater tot thoughtfully. I get why

this is Micah's favorite truck. "Elise and I are fighting, and it's stressing me out. We've never even had an argument before."

"So you're mad at her?" Micah cocks his head. I wonder if he ever fought with his friends in Tacoma.

"Yeah, a little. Maybe." Now that I think about it, I'm not sure I *am* angry with Elise. I wipe away the sweat dripping down my hairline. "I guess . . . I'm sad Elise isn't happier for me. I'm annoyed she started this nonsense in the first place. And I'm confused because I don't totally understand why she's angry."

"You don't know why she's angry?"

"Uhh . . ." I wasn't expecting to discuss my friendship drama with Micah. I thought today would be the perfect break from that stress. But Micah is genuinely interested. I think of how best to explain our disagreement.

"She's mostly mad because I got Brigitta. That was her dream role, and Elise can be pretty passionate about theater. But she's been mean to me ever since, which isn't fair. And then we said some not-so-nice things to each other at the movie screening."

"So you *do* know why she's angry." Micah points a tater tot at me.

"You sound like my therapist." I point my cheesecake skewer back at him.

"Seriously?" Micah's mouth drops open, revealing a

disgusting mix of mashed potato and sour cream. "That's what I want to be when I grow up. Some kind of therapist or psychology person."

"Really?"

"Yeah." Micah pauses to shovel down more food. He may be kinder than most boys our age, but his eating habits are unfortunately typical. "When I was younger, I liked talking a lot. Well, I still do. I asked my mom if there was a job where I could get paid to talk to people. You know, really talk to people and listen to them and stuff. And she said I should be a therapist."

"I think you would be an amazing therapist," I say as I swallow the last bit of cheesecake. Micah is definitely a good talker—and listener, as I've learned—but there's also something calming about his presence. Like Ariel, he makes me feel comfortable being myself. I don't have to pretend I'm okay when I'm not.

"Sorry, I didn't mean to bore you with all my issues. I'm totally happy hanging out with you instead of her," I say brightly. "Tell me. Are you fighting with any lifelong BFFs? Can I help you talk through any problems?"

"Sadly, I don't have many friends in Minnesota to fight with." Micah laughs, but it's a sad laugh.

"I'm sorry."

Elise and I may not be speaking, but at least I have Fatima. And the other theater kids. And my student council friends at school. I can't imagine moving across the country and leaving everyone behind. I nudge his shoulder with my own. Then the thought flits through my brain: *This is how a girlfriend would respond.* That makes me nervous, though, so I hop to my feet.

"Do you want to show me around?" I ask.

"Of course. I'll tell you all the truck gossip."

I follow Micah to a metal trash can, where he throws away his leftover tots. Next to me, a small Jack Russell terrier lifts his leg to pee on the side. I jump backward, shrieking, and toss my plate in the right direction. It bounces off the side, which means I have to duck around the peeing dog to avoid littering. We're both cracking up as we dash away from the confused dog and his disgruntled human.

For the rest of the afternoon, Micah and I walk in laps around the festival, occasionally stopping for strawberry lemonade or edible cookie dough. He insists on paying every time, even when I race to get my money first. It's definitely how a boyfriend would behave. The girl at the cookie dough truck winks when she hands over my cup of double chocolate chip, and I can hear my friends in my brain:

It's sexist if a boy always pays for you, Elise would say. *That's not gender equality.*

Or maybe he's just being nice, Fatima would counter. *I think it's sweet.*

That's when I realize I kinda lied to Micah earlier. I am having a great time hanging out with him. That part is true. But he can't replace a friend like Elise. Nobody can. If I've learned anything from teen movies, it's that the best thing about having a boyfriend is getting to talk about him with your friends. And right now, that part is missing.

FAILING

"Shannon!" Mom's voice echoes from downstairs. "Dinner in ten minutes! Can you set the table?"

"Yeah!" I yell back.

I'm sitting on the edge of my trundle bed with my penguin slippers planted firmly on the shag rug. When Fatima gave me these slippers for my birthday last year, I thought the fuzzy, black-and-white birds were adorable. Today, their beady eyes mock me.

I lied to Ariel again during our session this week. I planned to come clean, to admit that I've struggled with every single exposure exercise so far—except the Chap-Stick assignment that Grandma Ruby helped me with, of course—but I couldn't handle disappointing her. I love how happy she gets when I succeed at a difficult task. Her eyebrows shoot up and she clasps her hands together like I'm sharing the best news ever.

My task this week is to lie down on the bed with my penguin slippers still attached to my feet. When I told Ariel I always, always, *always* wear clean socks in bed, she decided this would be an exciting challenge. As if contaminating my entire bed with dust and bug guts could ever be exciting.

Yes, my slippers are my cleanest shoes. And yes, my bedroom floor gets mopped twice a week—once by Mom and once by me. But allowing the rubber soles to physically touch my pristine sheets is a risk I've never taken before.

I slide my right foot off the rug, onto the wood, and toward the mattress. I shudder. That was a mistake. I probably made the penguin slipper dirtier. I switch tactics, picking up my left foot instead. I feel ridiculous with my leg hovering a few inches above the ground, but I don't have any better ideas. Like when I tried to step inside my bedroom wearing my Vans, there's an invisible force field keeping the penguin slipper where it belongs.

I'm not sure *what* will happen if a dirty shoe touches my bed. But it feels big and scary and permanent. Like I might ruin the peace and comfort of my bedroom forever.

I kick off my slippers and lie down, pulling out my cell phone. Ever since our afternoon at the food truck festival,

Micah and I have been texting back and forth—random jokes about theater, pictures of his three cats, and pointless comments about the weather. With Elise still giving me the silent treatment and Fatima busy with the techies, it's nice to have someone reliable to chat with. I open his latest text.

> **Micah:** A thief snuck into a theater on opening night. He stole the spotlight.

I send back a series of eye-roll emojis before opening a new message from Fatima. I texted her after rehearsal to ask if she wanted to see a movie this weekend. Once again, she took hours to respond.

> **Fatima:** I don't know if I have time. Mrs. Davis needs help finishing the costumes, and I promised to help.

> **Me:** That's okay. The musical comes first!

> **Fatima:** No, I feel bad for being so busy. Maybe we can meet at the park for a little while? Tomorrow?

> **Me:** That's perfect! It's only Maria and Captain von Trapp rehearsing.

Mom yells my name again from downstairs. "Five minutes until dinner!" I hear a noise that sounds like Grandma Ruby grunting in displeasure.

Eating dinner used to be my favorite part of the day because (1) food is awesome, (2) the dining room usually smells like all-purpose cleaner, and (3) dinner is when Mom and I would discuss our emotions in great detail. I even liked having dinner back when Grandma Ruby first moved in. It was a big adjustment, but I secretly enjoyed her ridiculous life lessons and dramatic anecdotes. Things have only gotten worse between Mom and Grandma Ruby, though. I'm expecting fifteen minutes of silently eating chicken pot pie before I can reasonably ask to be excused.

"I'm coming in a second!" I shout back. "I'm doing a therapy exercise."

I toss my phone aside, shove my feet back into the slippers, and attempt the task again. *Just one second on the bed,* I tell myself. *It's not a big deal.*

Still, my feet falter when they're inches from the sheets. The black rubber beaks tremble as I struggle to lift my legs any farther. I squeeze my eyes shut, visualizing my feet touching the bed. When I open my eyes again, my slippers haven't moved, and I can tell the penguins are laughing at me. I don't know what's worse—that I can't complete a simple assignment or that I believe inanimate shoes are mocking me. It's all humiliating.

With a sigh, I heave myself off the trundle bed. Ariel's assignment will have to wait until tomorrow. I run a brush through my hair, then switch shoes in the hallway. The house is filled with the smell of melting cheese and the noise of sizzling fat. So I was wrong about dinner. It'll be fifteen minutes of silently eating cheeseburgers, not chicken pot pie.

Lucky me.

●●●●●●

We meet at a park near Fatima's house this time. It's one of those ultramodern ones that feels more like a circus than a neighborhood park. The ground is covered in bits of blue and black rubber and the playground equipment looks like spaceships ready for takeoff. There's a sensory table for the little ones and a rock-climbing wall for older kids, but basic necessities are missing. There are no swings. There is no slide. I don't think it should even count as a park.

Fatima and I climb to the top of the largest spaceship, avoiding the swarm of elementary schoolers dashing across the rubber. We sit on a red platform—where I imagine the cockpit would be—and dangle our legs off the edge. Across the park, Mom waves from a shaded picnic bench. Grandma Ruby was busy organizing her stamp collection, so Mom offered to drive us. I'm grateful I won't have to share my friend with my theater-obsessed grandma today.

"Omigod, that is so adorable! I can't believe you spent five hours together. That's my dream." Fatima sighs wistfully and stares at a maple tree in the distance. She's always been a romantic.

"Sometimes I didn't know what to say, which was awkward. But it was mostly fun." I pause for a second. "And he's really cute." I make a sound that's a little too close to a giggle for my liking.

"Totally," Fatima agrees.

Beneath us, the younger kids are shrieking and scrambling around the play structure. One boy in neon green—he looks bigger than the rest—is stomping and growling, reaching for the ankles of the other kids. It reminds me of the game Fatima, Elise, and I used to play at recess with the other girls in our grade. One of us—usually Elise because she was so tall—would be the lava monster. The rules were simple: Don't touch the lava and don't get caught by the lava monster. As I watch the kid in green lunge for his friend's tennis shoe, I long for the simplicity of elementary school. There were never any fights, never any drama. At least not with my friends.

"Hey, so have you seen Elise lately? Any news on whether she wants to be friends with me again?" I try to sound lighthearted, like our broken relationship is something to joke about, but my voice catches on the last word.

"I've been super busy. You know . . . so much time at the theater." Fatima bites her bottom lip and fiddles with the gold ring on her middle finger. It's obvious she's hiding something.

"You can tell me," I say. "I really don't mind. I know you're still friends."

"Okay . . ." Fatima continues messing with her ring. I apply ChapStick and brace myself for whatever she's about to say. "Well, we really haven't talked about you. It's awkward for me to be in the middle, you know?"

"Yeah, I get it." I stare across the park at my mom. She's hunched over whatever book she brought from home.

"But we have hung out a few times," Fatima says. "Actually, we should talk about plans for my half-birthday. When Elise and I were at the movies last week, she mentioned possibly . . ."

Wait a second. Yesterday, when I asked if she wanted to see a movie, Fatima claimed she was too busy with the show. But she had enough time for Elise? My fingers clench my thighs until my nails leave tiny divots in the soft skin. The thought of Fatima choosing Elise over me makes me want to throw up. She knows Elise was the one who started acting weird. That means I should come first, right?

Right?

I force myself to take a deep breath. Maybe Fatima had more free time last week. Now it's almost tech week and that means crunch time for everyone, especially the techies. But still, Elise got a full movie date with Fatima while all I get is a measly hour at the park. I'm more angry at Elise than ever. If she can't handle being my friend, then whatever. But stealing Fatima for herself? I never imagined she would do something so mean.

"Shannon, did you hear what I said?" Fatima sounds annoyed.

"Yeah. You and Elise went to the movies. I heard you." I keep my voice level.

"No, I was talking about ..." Fatima sighs. "Never mind."

The horde of kids on the playground have switched to a fancy version of tag. I can't tell the rules from up here, but there seems to be more skipping and singing than normal. I remember Bethany Anderson's birthday party in fourth grade when her mom made us play musical chairs even though Bethany told her we were too old. Elise got so competitive that she knocked over Sydney Bala before triumphantly sliding her butt onto a chair. I now feel a delayed surge of empathy for Sydney, who moved at the end of that year. She was playing a simple party game when Elise pushed her down. I know the feeling.

"I should get going," Fatima says. "Do you think your mom could drop me off at the theater?"

"Probably, yeah." I knew Fatima didn't have much time, but our hour together flew by. "I still need your advice, though. What am I supposed to do about Micah?" My voice sounds whinier than I'd like.

"What do you mean?" Fatima stands up and swings onto the circular monkey bars before hopping off. I take the easier path—a metallic spiral staircase—and meet her on the ground. "He obviously likes you."

"I know . . . or I think I know. But how can I tell if he wants to be my boyfriend? Is there some way to ask him without embarrassing myself?"

"Huh. I'm not sure. Maybe we can talk about it later?" Fatima asks.

"Yeah, okay," I say as we move within earshot of the picnic tables. Mom looks up from her book and waves. I try to sound happy, even though I know the odds of getting my only friend alone are slim. "Later sounds good."

AWKWARD SILENCE

Nobody is talking to anybody.

At home, Mom and Grandma Ruby are still mad. They barely speak to each other anymore—just the occasional muttered "pass the salt" or "is it necessary to cough that much?"—so I can't tell what they're fighting about.

It's more of the same at rehearsal. Elise isn't talking to me, obviously, and Fatima always disappears into the set shop before I can say hello. After being rejected by Amir, Adeline isn't speaking to anyone, but she *especially* isn't talking to Naomi, who she somehow blames. Even little Sara and Riya are glaring at each other with crossed arms.

Today is our first full run-through of the show, so all the techies are too busy for idle conversation. They're running around, frantically arranging props, debating sound cues, and messing with the lights.

"All right." Mr. Bryant claps a few times. "Quiet down, people," he adds out of habit. The auditorium isn't buzzing with its usual noisy chatter. "Take a seat. I want to explain how today is going to work."

Amir plops into the chair next to me, probably because the older girls are ignoring him. He's wearing a pink T-shirt that says, "I'm not yelling, I'm projecting." It would be funnier if everything wasn't so depressing.

I'm glancing back and forth between Micah, who waves when I make eye contact, and Elise, who sat as far away from me as possible. I'm at a loss for words with both of them, which is seriously unlike me. Normally, I would have a multistep plan in place, but all I've got is a sick feeling in my gut.

With Elise, I'm tempted to apologize because I know I said some not-so-nice things. But I think she should apologize too. She's the one who ended our friendship because I dared to audition for the musical and not totally suck. The problem is that I don't want to apologize if Elise doesn't. That feels like admitting I'm the only one who's wrong, which I definitely am not.

For Micah, it's the opposite. Everything is amazing between us. We laugh, we joke, we hold hands when nobody's watching—but I need to know what that means. Maybe some girls wouldn't care about the definition, but I'm Shannon Carter. I'm not known for being easygoing. My brain needs to have everything sorted into tidy boxes.

"Does that make sense to everyone?"

I barely listened to Mr. Bryant's instructions. This may be my first time acting, but it's not my first show. I know we'll be performing the musical from start to finish with lighting, sound effects, and all the props that are finished. Mrs. Davis will oversee everything in the sound booth while Mr. Bryant will be backstage with us. It's not technically a dress rehearsal because our costumes aren't ready, but it's close to the real thing.

I quickly text Mom and tell her rehearsal might run late—the show is over two hours long—then join the other von Trapp kids in the hallway behind the stage. We're allowed to whisper when the stage door is closed, but nobody has much to say. Micah and I chat about boring things like what we ate for lunch, but I'm not going to say anything *real* with everyone else around. The closest we get is sharing a smile when Micah mentions the cat picture he sent me last night. Other than that, the hallway is quiet. The tension is kinda uncomfortable, so I'm relieved, rather than nervous, when our first entrance arrives.

Once I'm onstage, the time whizzes by. Auditioning for the musical may have ruined my friendship with Elise, but I don't think I regret it. Mostly because I love playing Brigitta. The singing and dancing is fun, but what's best is simply taking a break from being Shannon. As Brigitta, I get to be confident and funny and strong-willed—all the things I wish I could be in real life. In fact, I almost start crying when we sing the final notes of "Climb Every Mountain" and the house lights come back on. It's like being transported back to a less exciting and more stressful reality.

"I'll see you tomorrow?" Micah asks when we're packing up to leave.

"Of course. Hey, um . . ." I want to be bold and ask for him to officially be my boyfriend, but then I see Elise standing a few feet away. What if she makes fun of me? Or spreads some kind of rumor about me asking out a boy? She never would have betrayed me before, but everything is different now.

"What's up?" Micah asks.

"Uh, n-nothing," I stammer. "I forgot, I mean. But I'll see you tomorrow?"

"Sure. Great job today." Micah grins and runs down the aisle. So much for being bold.

I unlock my phone and see two voice mails and a bunch of missed calls from Mom. I press the phone to my ear and listen to the most recent one. It turns out she's stuck in a meeting, so I need to find a ride home.

I throw the rest of my stuff into my backpack and sprint out of the near-empty auditorium. If Fatima and Amir leave without me, I'll be stuck here. Or worse, I'll have to ride with some random kid's parent.

I burst through the glass doors, momentarily blinded

by the harsh sunlight, but then I spot Amir's dirty Toyota at the far end of the parking lot. I run through the pickup lane, not bothering to look both ways, and I'm panting by the time I reach the car. After a few knocks, Amir rolls down the window.

"Shannon, are you okay?"

"Hey, sorry. Is it possible to get a ride? My mom can't come."

"Of course," Amir says; then his face becomes solemn. "I shall have you home at once, my child."

"Um, okay?"

The passenger seat is covered in books, so I circle around to the backseat. I open the door and am greeted by a smiling Fatima. I expected that. What I didn't expect was a scowling Elise sitting next to her. Of course Elise is with her. They've been riding together most days, which I would have remembered if I'd stopped to think. I can't believe Elise is getting movie trips *and* car rides with Fatima. That's totally unfair. Fatima scoots into the middle seat to make room for me, but I'm frozen outside the open door.

"Is everything okay, my child?" Amir's weirdness shakes me out of my awkward stupor. I slide in next to Fatima and squish my backpack at my feet.

"Yeah, I'm good." I buckle my seat belt as Amir pulls out of the parking space. "Did he just call me his child?" I ask Fatima.

"Yes." She rolls her eyes. "He's started staying in character outside of rehearsal. Which is super, duper, ANNOYING!" She shouts the last word at Amir and shakes his shoulder. It's not the safest choice to harass someone while they're driving, but she probably can't help it. Living with a fake Captain von Trapp can't be easy.

"That sounds strange," I say.

"Omigod, you have no idea." Fatima groans. "He's started whistling whenever he wants to get my attention. I feel like I'm living with a drill sergeant."

"I'm a retired naval officer, not a drill sergeant," Amir says. "Precision is of the utmost importance when discussing your elders."

"You're only five years older than me. And you're a part-time piano teacher, not a retired navy whatever." Fatima rolls her eyes again. "He even refused to go out with Adeline because it would affect 'the believability of their father/daughter relationship.'" She uses air quotes on this last bit.

"Wait, what?" I stare at Amir. "You blew off Adeline because she's playing Liesl?"

"Obviously," Amir says. "She's sixteen going on seventeen, after all. It would be wholly inappropriate to be romantic with my own child."

"She's not your child!" Fatima yells. "She's literally older than you!"

I burst into laughter. I've missed riding with Amir. His antics always get more ridiculous as opening night approaches. I glance at Elise, who's staring stubbornly out the window. I can't believe she's refusing to even laugh with us. Anger surges through me. It's not fair that she basically claimed carpooling with Fatima. I know her dads work full-time during the summer, but still. These car rides used to be one of my favorite parts of the day, and she's stolen that from me.

"You remember my half-birthday is coming up, right?" Fatima asks.

"Of course," I say, though I'd honestly forgotten with everything else going on. Elise doesn't bother responding, even though we're supposed to be planning this party together.

"Okay." Fatima looks back and forth between me and Elise, her eyes wide with worry. "I know things have been weird or whatever, but it can still be fun. Maybe if we invite some more friends, then . . ."

I can barely focus on anything Fatima's saying. I'm so infuriated by Elise's disregard that it's consuming every muscle in my body. My hands are balled into fists at my sides. I can feel blood rushing to my head. Inside my boots, my toes are clenched.

". . . I was thinking laser tag or one of those bouncy things, but maybe that's too childish . . ."

I'm glad I didn't apologize to Elise during rehearsal. She doesn't deserve an apology from me. Not after everything she's done. So what if I said a few mean things? She's been treating me like garbage this entire summer. All because I had the nerve to be a decent singer. What kind of friend is that?

". . . It might be too hot for an ice cream cake if we're outside, so we could do something simple like . . ."

And now she's stolen Fatima and Amir and half the girls in the musical, leaving me with who? A boy I'm too scared to ask out and a handful of people I barely know? That's not fair at all. She's the one who started this whole mess, so I should get to keep our friends.

"Uh, Shannon?" Fatima waves her hand in front of my face. "Are you listening?"

"Yeah," I snap. Even that makes me mad. How come Fatima is asking if *I'm* listening when Elise has been ignoring us this entire car ride? I try to make my voice a little nicer. "Sorry, what did you say?"

"We're at your house," Fatima says.

"Oh, right." I grab my backpack and push open the car door with more force than necessary.

"Take care, Brigitta! Remember that your bedtime is eight o'clock sharp!" Amir says.

That should make me smile, but it doesn't. Nothing does anymore.

ARIEL THE MERMAID

" How are you doing?"

"This is the worst week of my entire life." I'm lying on Ariel's couch, staring at a water stain on the ceiling. Sitting upright seemed like too much effort today.

"Worse than last week?"

"I don't even remember last week." I press a velvet throw pillow into my face and breathe deeply. The fabric smells faintly of cigarette smoke and flowers. Before this summer, I would have been disgusted, but now the smell of smoke reminds me of Grandma Ruby. It's almost comforting.

"How is the situation with your mother and grandmother?" Ariel asks.

"Bad."

"And how about with your friends?"

"Bad."

That's a massive understatement. The situation with Elise and Fatima has gotten worse, which I didn't think was possible. Yesterday, I overheard Elise whispering about me with some of the nuns. Who knows what horrible rumor she's spreading? And when I told Fatima what happened, she seemed annoyed with me.

"I'm sorry to hear that."

I peek at Ariel from behind my pillow. She's watching me carefully, her forehead wrinkled. She looks super worried, like it's her fault my life sucks. I toss the pillow aside, swing my legs onto the floor, and slowly pull myself up. "Sorry," I say. "It's been a hard week."

"You've been having a lot of those recently."

"Yeah." That's another understatement.

"What about the boy you're spending time with?"

"Micah's good." I smile. I've made no progress on the boyfriend issue, but it's a relief to have one person who doesn't hate spending time with me.

"Well, another thing that *has* been going well is your exposure therapy, right?" Ariel slips off her flats and tucks her legs next to her. As usual, I try to think about anything but her bare feet. "How did the slipper exercise go? Were you able to put them on your sheets?"

"Fine." I bounce my fist against my thigh, three times on the left and three times on the right. I think about my penguin slippers staring at me with their beady eyes. Mocking me. Laughing at my failure.

"That's outstanding, Shannon!" Ariel beams. "What an achievement. You've committed to doing the work and look at these results! I'm so proud of you."

"Well, don't be." Ariel's praise makes me squirm. She's acting like I won a Nobel Peace Prize or something when all I've done, week after week, is lie. "It's not a big deal. I'm still a mess."

"I don't know if that's true." Ariel pauses, and I get the sense she's waiting for me to say something more. Instead, I keep staring at the floor. "Don't forget all your previous successes, Shannon. These assignments may seem small, but it's important to celebrate your victories."

"Yeah, whatever." I slump down into the couch. I'm exhausted. There's too much going wrong in my life, and my brain is working overtime trying to keep up. I don't have the energy to keep lying to Ariel. I'm not sure why I started lying in the first place. It's just a therapy assignment. She must have clients more messed up than me who fail at this stuff all the time.

"Shannon? I can't tell what's happening in your brain unless you tell me." Ariel leans in. "You *can* tell me. I'm here for you."

"Really?" A bark of laughter escapes from my throat. "What if I told you I've lied about every single assignment you gave me? Well, not the ChapStick because of my grandmother, but the other ones. I didn't walk in my bedroom wearing the wrong shoes. I couldn't put my slippers on my bed. Maybe I could if I tried, but I barely tried. It's too much, okay?"

I'm staring at my feet, at the ceiling, at the blank wall. Anything to avoid looking at Ariel. I can't tell if she's angry or disappointed or sad, but now that I've started truth-telling, I can't stop. There's a massive river of feelings rushing through me, and the dam just broke.

"I just need something to be easy! Is that too much to ask? But every single thing in my life sucks. And when I try to make it better, it somehow gets suckier!" I stomp my foot against the floor so hard a wave of pain shoots up my shin. "I need Grandma Ruby and Mom to stop fighting so much. And I need Mom to stop asking if I really want to do the musical. It's *so* annoying. I can't stand it. And I need Elise to stop being mad at me. And I need her to stop stealing Fatima. Or maybe I need Fatima to choose me. I don't know. I just need something to go right. I need . . ."

My shouted words turn into gasped breaths, then heaving sobs. I double over on the couch, clutching my knees, rocking back and forth. I expect Ariel to hug me, to comfort me like Mom always does, but she doesn't move from her chair. Maybe she's still thinking about all the lies I told her.

When I finally glance up, Ariel doesn't look angry. She doesn't look surprised or confused either. For once, I can't tell what she's feeling. All she does is push a box of tissues toward me. I grab a handful and blow my nose, making an obscenely loud honk.

"Do you feel better?" Ariel asks. It seems like an absurd question at first, but then I realize I do. Completely freaking out has calmed me down. I feel the same sort of peace I did while playing games with Grandma Ruby.

"Yeah, actually."

"Good." Ariel studies me, snapping her hair clip open and closed. Then she stands, slides her feet back into her flats, and starts roaming around the room. She grabs a few books from a shelf, a picture frame from her desk, then the yellow fish statue I noticed before. My eyes are heavy, and I let them blink shut while Ariel fetches an armful of random items. Finally, she plucks the tiny crab from the pile of fidgets and places everything on the table between us.

"I have a thing for *The Little Mermaid*." That statement makes my eyes fly open. Of all the ways Ariel could respond to my meltdown, this is *so* not what I expected. "Have you noticed that?"

"Yeah," I say. "I mean, kind of." In front of me are twenty or thirty different objects, all decorated with characters or scenes from the movie. Books, snow globes, coffee mugs, even an Ursula-themed flashlight. It's impossible not to notice. I've spent hours thinking about the combination of Ariel's name, her red hair, and the suspicious number of sea creatures in her office. But looking at the array in front of me, I realize I've missed most of the *Little Mermaid* merchandise. Ariel is a hard-core collector.

"My hair isn't naturally this color," she says, sitting back in her chair, which doesn't surprise me. I didn't think people could achieve that level of red naturally. "I colored it when my brother passed away."

I stare at Ariel, shocked. She's never told me anything about her personal life—I thought that was some rule therapists had to follow—and the first thing she shares is that her brother died?

"I was born three years after Rob, and my parents let him pick my name. Toddlers shouldn't have that much responsibility." Ariel smiles a sad kind of smile. "But Rob was obsessed with Disney, and *The Little Mermaid* was his absolute favorite. He wanted to name me Ariel.

"My parents went along with it, though they changed the pronunciation. I think the name is part of why Rob and I were so close. We watched Disney movies together every weekend and reenacted them for our parents. Unlike my friends' siblings, Rob never stopped wanting to hang out with me as we grew older. Sometimes he even chose a movie night with me over a party with his friends. He was my favorite person in the entire world.

"During my senior year of high school, Rob was killed by a drunk driver. It was right before Christmas break, and he was driving home from college. I had been invited to go skiing with my friend's family the next week, and I told my parents I still wanted to go. They tried to stop me, but I insisted I was fine. I wasn't feeling sad. I wasn't feeling anything, really. My whole body was numb. I knew I needed to escape all the crying relatives and frozen lasagnas.

"My parents shouldn't have let me go, but they did. Maybe they thought getting away would be good for me. So four days after my brother died, I flew to Aspen with my best friend and her family. I pretended like everything was fine, which it kind of was. We went skiing and drank hot chocolate and watched movies. I was doing well until one night, when my friend suggested we watch *The Little Mermaid*, I completely lost it.

"I started sobbing and screaming and I left my friend's family without telling them where I was going. My plan was to get a cab to the airport, but I found a car in front of the hotel with the keys in the ignition. I took it—well, no. I *stole* the car and was driving to the airport when I saw a beauty salon. I ran inside, pulled out the wad of cash my parents had given me, and told them I wanted my hair bright red. The police found me a few hours later, but it was too late for my hair. I've been a redhead ever since.

"My parents flew out the next day to bring me home.

After that, I didn't leave my room for months. I had to redo my senior year of high school. The only time I saw daylight was when my parents dragged me to therapy or I had an appointment to get my roots touched up."

Ariel finishes her story and wipes a few tears from her eyes. I feel uncomfortable, like when I see a teacher in the grocery store. I never imagined Ariel having a real life outside of her office. I certainly didn't imagine her having such a hard life. At worst, I assumed *The Little Mermaid* mementos were a strange quirk, not a tribute to her brother.

"Are you allowed to tell me things like that?" I ask. I know that's not how you're supposed to react to someone sharing the saddest moment of their life, but it's the only question I can think of.

"Probably not." Ariel stretches out her legs and wiggles her toes. "My point is . . . we all lose control sometimes, Shannon. It's okay to not be okay. Because you know what?"

"What?"

"Life really sucks sometimes." Ariel smiles. "It doesn't suck all the time. And it sucks different amounts for different people. But you can't avoid the suckiness altogether."

"That's your advice?" I stare at her. What happened to my super-professional, super-kind, super-helpful therapist?

"No, that's just the truth. But I suppose it's my job to

give you *some* kind of advice . . ." Ariel laughs, and I crack a smile too. "Listen, Shannon. When Rob died, I was totally lost. I didn't know how to grieve. I didn't know what I needed."

"I don't know what I need either."

"Of course you do." Ariel starts stacking books and putting away the *Little Mermaid* trinkets. We're close to running out of time. "A little while ago, you told me. You need your grandmother to be nicer. You need your mom to stop doubting you . . ." Ariel continues reciting the list I only half remember shouting.

"Well, yeah," I say when she's done reminding me of everything wrong in my life. "That would all be great, but how do I make those things happen?"

"You ask." Ariel shrugs. "Especially with your family. You say, 'Here's how I'm struggling, and here's what I need.'"

"And that's supposed to work?" I try to picture how Grandma Ruby would react to a statement like that.

"It's worth a try." Ariel shrugs again. "Or you can follow my example and ignore all of your emotions until you freak out and steal a car. The choice is yours."

FAMILY MEETING

"How was therapy?" Mom asks.

"Fine." I adjust the recline of the passenger seat. I can always tell when Grandma Ruby has been in the car, because she sits totally upright like she's taking a test or flying a plane. "Ariel said some interesting stuff."

"Good! Did she have any advice about your friends?"

"Sorta. She said I should tell people what problems I'm having and how we can fix them. But I kinda think that would make Elise more mad. I'd have to phrase it differently, you know?"

"That makes sense." Mom fiddles with the radio until she finds a station that isn't playing a commercial. "I think being up front is always smart."

"You do?" I watch Mom's expression as she concentrates

on the road. I haven't told her Ariel suggested doing the exact same thing with her and Grandma Ruby.

"Absolutely," Mom says as she flips on her blinker. "Much better than keeping all that stress inside."

* * * * * *

When we get home, I grab a banana and run upstairs. I can worry about Ariel's advice later. For now, I need to review my lines in a serious way. I stumbled on two of them and completely forgot one today. I think it's just nerves, but with dress rehearsals coming up, I can't be making silly mistakes. I switch shoes in the hallway, then head into my bedroom.

I'm walking toward my desk when I trip over a suitcase. An open suitcase. A suitcase that smells an awful lot like cigarettes.

I look to the closet. Grandma Ruby is yanking clothes off hangers and tossing them onto the floor. She pulls open a drawer and throws balls of pantyhose in my direction. She doesn't say anything, but I know she heard me come in. What I don't know is why she's tearing apart my bedroom.

"Um, Grandma Ruby? What's going on?"

"I'm packing." Her voice is crisp. She flings a bathrobe in my direction.

"I see that." I step over a pile of worn-out sandals. "I thought the repairs on your house were delayed again."

"They are. But I'm still leaving." Grandma Ruby looks up. "Shannon, this isn't about you, okay? You're my only granddaughter, and I've always wanted to spend more time together."

"So then why are you packing?!" I'm looking around the room for some clue about what happened between this morning—when Grandma Ruby was happily eating a bagel at our table—and right now. But all I see are clothes strewn everywhere.

"Andrea has made it clear that I'm not needed." Grandma Ruby sniffs. "I don't want to intrude any longer."

"But I like having you here!"

I may not have been enthusiastic about Grandma Ruby moving into my bedroom, but I've grown to love her snide comments and sarcastic humor. She and Mom have their issues but that's not a good reason for her to leave.

"Grandma, stop packing. Please? One little fight isn't a big deal."

"Sorry, Shannon. I think it's best if I move into a hotel for the time being." Grandma Ruby turns back to the closet and pulls more clothing off hangers. Her mind is made up.

"Mom!" I yell. No answer. I lean into the hallway, my penguin slippers planted in the bedroom, and bellow down the stairs. "MOM!"

"Shannon? What's wrong?" I hear hurried footsteps; then Mom appears. "What's happening, sweetie?"

"It's Grandma Ruby," I say. Mom kicks off her shoes and joins me in the bedroom. "She's packing all her stuff."

"What the—" Mom surveys the wreckage that is my bedroom. She kicks the suitcase shut and steps toward Grandma Ruby. "Mother, what is going on?"

"Like I told Shannon, it's clear I'm not wanted here."

"Is this because of our argument earlier today?" Mom sighs. "Come on, Mother. Don't be so dramatic."

"I'm not being dramatic. I'm being practical," Grandma Ruby says. "I don't want to impose any longer. My presence is disrupting your household. You've made that abundantly clear."

"All I did was ask you to not smoke inside!"

I close my eyes and lean against the door frame. I may have missed this particular argument, but I've been around for plenty. Mom criticizes Grandma Ruby. Grandma Ruby criticizes Mom. They both get defensive and start yelling and bringing up things from before I was born. The whole thing is totally preventable and yet it keeps happening day after day.

"Can you guys listen for a minute?" My quiet plea goes unheard. Grandma Ruby is pacing back and forth in front of the closet, wringing her hands. Mom is on the verge of tears. "Seriously! Stop yelling and—"

It's no use. Once they're this far into it, I'm basically invisible. I'm about to leave the room when Ariel's words pop into my head.

Tell them what you need.

They might be the grown-ups in the room, but they're not acting like it. I clear my throat. "I have something to say." Mom glances at me, but Grandma Ruby keeps ranting. "I SAID I HAVE SOMETHING TO SAY!"

The sound of somebody else yelling breaks Grandma Ruby out of her spell. She and Mom both look at me, dumbfounded. I don't think I've ever screamed that loudly before in my life. And it's not like anyone can chastise me because yelling is all Mom and Grandma Ruby have been doing this summer.

"That's better." I smile pleasantly. "We're having a family meeting in five minutes."

"What's that now?" Mom asks.

"I *said* we're having a family meeting in five minutes. In the living room. Bring your own snacks."

* * *

Four minutes and thirty seconds later, Mom and Grandma Ruby are sitting on the couch. Mom had grabbed a bottle of wine from the kitchen and two glasses for her and Grandma Ruby. It's not quite what I meant by snacks, but whatever. I hold up a wooden napkin ring. I came prepared too.

"This is the Talking Napkin Ring," I say.

"Huh?" Mom tilts her head, confused.

"Andrea, your daughter is losing it," Grandma Ruby whispers loudly.

In my language arts class last year, my teacher had a plush taco that was almost definitely meant to be a dog toy. She called it the "Talking Taco," and we used it exclusively during class discussions. The rule was simple: Only the person who held the Talking Taco could speak. Its purpose was to prevent the overprepared students (like Fatima) and the overeager students (like Elise) from talking over each other. It worked surprisingly well for something on sale at Petco.

Unfortunately, I don't have a plush taco, so this napkin ring will have to do. I explain the process to Mom and Grandma Ruby, who nod along. They clearly agreed to humor me at this unexpected family meeting. I guess agreeing about anything is a good start.

"I've called the first ever Carter Family Meeting to discuss Grandma Ruby's decision to move out." I pick at the scratched wood of the napkin ring. "I think her leaving is a bad idea," I say. "Because the musical opens in one week, and I still need help with my lines. Also because hotels are expensive. Also because I like having a cribbage partner."

"Shannon—" Mom tries to say something, but Grandma Ruby cuts her off.

"Hush, Andrea. You don't have the Talking Napkin Ring."

Mom smiles at this interruption and holds up her hands in apology.

"And it's more than that . . ." I grip the napkin ring tightly. Ariel's advice made so much sense in her office, but now it seems hard. It shouldn't be, though. This is my mom and my grandma. I should be able to tell them what I'm feeling. I shake out my hair and straighten my back. I feel like I'm onstage, auditioning for the musical. Everyone is watching me, waiting to see what I do next.

"In therapy today, Ariel and I were talking about how I can make things better if I tell people what I need. So . . ." I turn to Grandma Ruby. "I need you to stop criticizing my mom so much. It makes me feel sad and kinda angry." Grandma Ruby's eyebrows rise, and I backtrack a little. "I mean, it would be super great if you could be a little nicer. Especially when it's about me. Or maybe you could wait and argue in private? I'm always in the middle of your fights, and I don't like it."

I exhale shakily. There's a prickly pain in the back of my throat from trying not to cry. But I've come too far to give up now. And Ariel is right. It feels better to say what's on my mind.

"And, Mom." I turn to her. "Can you please, please, *please* stop asking if I'm sure about doing the musical? I know you're worried because of my OCD, but it makes me feel like you want me to quit. Or like you're waiting for me to fail. But I'm not failing. I'm good at acting and singing, actually. Well, the dancing is a little tough and I forgot some lines today and . . ."

I'm totally off topic now, so I decide to shut up. No matter what happens, I think Ariel would be proud of me. I watch Mom and Grandma Ruby carefully, waiting for their reactions. They look reasonably happy, but nobody's talking.

"So, uh, yeah." I glance between them. "No offense or anything. But that's how I'm feeling."

Still silence.

"Please say something," I say. "You're making me nervous."

"Per your rules, we cannot say something because we don't have the Talking Napkin Ring," Grandma Ruby says.

"Oh, right." I underestimated the power of this random object I grabbed from the kitchen table. I toss the napkin ring to Mom. She holds it carefully, like it's made of diamonds.

"I personally am very sorry for ever doubting you." Mom sniffs. "I can't make myself stop worrying, but I should have done a better job of supporting you. I'm just . . ." Mom hiccups, then sniffs again. "I'm just so darn proud of you, and I—" Her voice cracks as her eyes begin to glisten.

"Oh for Pete's sake. It's not the Crying Napkin Ring." Grandma Ruby grabs the wooden object from Mom's grasp. "I would also like to say that I'm very impressed by you, Shannon. I know your mom and I have been fighting, but that has nothing to do with you."

"I know, but—"

"As the *only* person with the power to speak right now"—she glares at me, but in a joking sort of way— "I promise we'll work on airing those disagreements in private. What do you think, Andrea?"

Mom is nodding and crying and drinking wine and smiling.

I can't stop smiling either. I don't know if it's their new promises or Mom's happy tears or Grandma Ruby's wholehearted embrace of the Talking Napkin Ring. Probably all three. But if I can make a little peace between two women who have spent their entire lives arguing, surely I can fix things with Elise.

COSTUME FITTING

On the Monday of tech week, I wake up before Grandma Ruby. Today is my big day.

Friday was supposed to be my big day, but Mr. Bryant called a last-minute rehearsal for the nuns. Apparently, the opening number is a mess. But that's okay. After a weekend of strategizing with Mom and playing cribbage with Grandma Ruby, I feel even more prepared to face Elise. Today is the day I get my friend back.

My plan is simple. I'm going to pull Elise aside and apologize. When Mom first suggested such an obvious solution, I protested. I didn't want to apologize first because Elise might not return the favor. We were both responsible for this whole blowup. (Her way more than me, if I'm being honest.) But Mom pointed out that someone has to make the first move. So I'm going to try that. Again.

I'm going to say sorry for all the mean things I said in the bathroom, and if Elise doesn't say sorry back . . . Well, I hope she does.

Today at rehearsal we're doing another full run-through and trying on costumes, so I'm supposed to be "stage ready," whatever that means. I attempt to braid my hair in two straight plaits—the hairstyle Mrs. Davis chose for Brigitta—but quickly give up and pull my hair into a messy bun. One of the older girls can braid my hair later. I wash my hands—three times, of course—and then my face. After brushing my teeth and putting on deodorant, I stare at myself in the mirror.

"You can do this," I say to Mirror Shannon. "You are capable. You are confident. If you can confront Mom and Grandma Ruby together, you can do anything. Today, you will take action."

My pep talk may have encouraged my brain, but my stomach isn't listening. I feel queasy as I eat a few spoon-fuls of Cheerios and sip on sparkling orange juice. The mild discomfort turns into serious nausea as we drive to rehearsal. By the time we arrive at the theater, I'm on the verge of vomiting.

"Don't forget to find a ride home. We're meeting with the contractors again." Mom squeezes my leg. "You've got this."

I nod and try a few deep breaths. Apparently, my lungs

weren't listening to the pep talk either. I want to wait in the car and stall a little longer, but the clock reads 9:28. And I have a feeling tardiness on the first day of tech week won't be appreciated.

The auditorium is total chaos. There are people shouting, techies running back and forth, and heaps of clothing strewn everywhere. It looks like a tornado blew through a department store from the 1930s—did they even *have* department stores back then?

"Sorry, Shannon!" Mrs. Davis yells. "There's a method to my madness, I swear. Cast is onstage."

"Thanks."

I look for Fatima among the piles of old-fashioned ball gowns and black robes. I was hoping for some words of encouragement, but I don't see her anywhere. I'm pretty sure she's on the costume committee, but I'm not positive. We haven't hung out since our day at the park, and it's been days since we've talked at all.

I wade through the mess, being careful not to step on anything. To my left, there's a stack of hideous yellow and green floral print rompers. I'm guessing those are the play clothes Maria makes from discarded curtains. On my right are folded brown pants and jackets, probably for the Nazis. And sitting atop a beige mannequin head is a bright pink wig that I'm quite certain is not for this show.

Onstage, there's even more commotion. Riya and Sara

are running around, admiring all the dresses. Micah and Robert are arguing about something. And there's a huge group of girls huddled around Amir's iPhone.

"Shannon, come here!" Naomi waves me over. "It's the flyer for our show."

"It was in the local newspaper!" Adeline yells.

I'm tempted to look, but I need to find Elise. I shake my head and wander backstage. I check the dressing rooms, the costume closet, and the back hallway. I peek into both restrooms and circle back around to the lobby. I've done a full loop of the theater, and there's no sign of either Elise or Fatima. Worry pricks at my brain. Are they off doing something without me? Or could something have happened to both of them?

When I make it back to the stage, the energy is somewhat calmer. Amir is showing the flyer to a group of techies, and Mr. Bryant is staring at the mess in the audience with disdain.

"What the he—" He looks at Sara, who's holding her hands over Riya's ears. "Sorry, sorry. What the *heck*, Evelyn? I thought you were going to be ready. I wanted to do costumes before the run-through."

"Well, we can't always get what we want, can we?" Mrs. Davis yells from a dark corner somewhere. If those two are in a relationship, it doesn't seem to be going well at the moment. "I need two more hours."

"Fine." Mr. Bryant huffs and turns back around. "Run-through first," he says to a collective groan. "Let's move, people. Places in five. I want a clean run, okay? And if you value my health at all, please stay on top of your entrances! If I see an empty stage, I'm going to have a heart attack, got it?"

Elise doesn't arrive until right before our first entrance. Amir and Naomi are finishing their scene together when she bursts through the double doors at the end of the back hallway. Her cheeks are pink and her face is covered in a thin layer of sweat.

"You're late," Adeline says.

"Sorry." Elise's voice is strained. "I didn't have a ride with Fatima, and my dads were at work. I wanted to get an Uber, but I'm too young so—"

"Shhh!" Robert whispers. "It's our cue."

"Why didn't you—"

A shrill whistle cuts me off, and all the von Trapp kids (except me) march onstage. I wanted to ask Elise why Amir didn't pick up her up since he's clearly at rehearsal, but now it's too late. I wait in the wings for another twenty seconds, then make my own entrance.

We don't have quite the squeaky-clean run Mr. Bryant asked for, but it's decent enough. True, Naomi slipped and almost fell down the fake stairs. Amir actually forgot a line. And the nuns messed up some choreography in spite of Friday's emergency rehearsal. But overall, it wasn't half bad.

Usually, after the show is finished, the entire cast sits on the edge of the stage while Mr. Bryant gives us notes— stuff that went well, stuff that could be better, stuff that he's certain the Northern Rep kids *aren't* struggling with. But not today. As soon as the audience lights come up, Mrs. Davis takes over. She starts calling names and handing out costumes with instructions to come see her once we're dressed.

Characters like the soldiers and the maids only have one costume, but the von Trapp children have five outfits each. For the girls, that means a gray sailor suit, a white nightgown, the ugly green-and-yellow romper, a sparkly party outfit, and an unremarkable blue dress. Plus a winter cloak for the finale. I take my stack of clothes from Mrs. Davis and follow everyone backstage.

I'm not sure of dressing room etiquette, but the other girls start changing clothes like it's the most natural thing in the world. I follow their lead, even though it feels the opposite of natural to undress in front of all these people. With so many outfits to try on, however, I quickly realize nobody's watching. I put on a costume, run to the auditorium, wait in line to be approved by Mrs. Davis, listen as she discusses all the ways she *could* improve the costume if only she had more time, and repeat.

Somehow, Elise ends up next to me, and we fall into a rhythm. Costume on, costume off. Costume on, costume off. As other kids head home for the day, I start to dawdle. Elise follows my lead. I wonder if she's thinking what I'm thinking. That once we're alone—or close to alone—in the dressing room, we can finally chat.

It's just me, Elise, and two other girls left when there's a loud knock on the door.

"Can I come in?" Mr. Bryant yells. "Is everyone decent?"

I look around as Elise yells, "Yeah!"

Mr. Bryant takes a small step inside. "Evelyn forgot to hand these out." He dumps a box of black shoes onto the counter. "They're all the same. Find a pair that fits, and you'll wear them for the entire show. Except the bedroom scene, obviously. I suppose the other girls can get them tomorrow."

I look at the haphazard pile of shoes. They're the old-fashioned style that little girls sometimes wear. Black leather. Low heel. A strap across the top. That's all fine.

What's not fine is my feet going inside them.

Mr. Bryant is still talking, but I don't hear him. All I can do is stare in horror at the filthiness of those shoes. The worn soles, frayed seams, and cracked leather. I can see specks of dirt and grime with my own eyes. I even spy what looks like a long-dead fly squished inside one of them.

I gasp and take an unsteady step backward. Wearing

somebody else's clothes is one thing. It's not great, but it's manageable. But letting my feet touch someone else's shoes? It's disgusting. It's horrifying. It's straight-up dangerous.

This is why I only wear three pairs of shoes.

This is why I don't do things like audition for the musical on a whim.

My heart is pounding, and I can feel myself start to hyperventilate. Thinking about my feet in those shoes is making my entire body feel dirty. My palms are sweaty. My armpits are damp. My lips are dry.

My lips are dry.

I shove my hands into my pockets and realize I'm still wearing the sailor outfit. I run to my pile of clothes, searching for the jean shorts I wore to rehearsal. My ChapStick is in the front left pocket of those shorts.

"Shannon!"

I throw clothing left and right, looking for the familiar shade of denim. They must be here somewhere. But with costumes piled everywhere and bags and makeup and—

"SHANNON!"

I look up. There's a blue and white tube of ChapStick in front of my face. I grab it without thinking and greedily run the balm across my lips. Three circles. Six circles. Nine circles. My breathing starts to slow and my heart rate returns to normal. I stand up, leaning against the counter for support. The dressing room is totally empty, except for me and Elise.

"You . . . you . . . ," I stammer. Elise looks embarrassed. "You had ChapStick. You had ChapStick for me."

"Yeah." She shrugs. "I always keep a spare tube with me. Just in case you need it."

My eyes fill with tears, and I throw my arms around Elise before my mind can overthink it. "The shoes were dirty." I'm crying into her sweaty hair, but I don't care. "The shoes were so dirty and I imagined putting them on my feet and I freaked out and . . ." Wait. Why am I blabbing on about shoes when there's something way more important I need to say. I pull back from the hug. "And I'm sorry."

"No." Elise shakes her head. "I'm the one who's sorry. I've been sorry for a long time."

"I mean, yeah," I say, and we both laugh. "But I can be sorry too."

There are so many things I want to say. Explanations I still need. A summer's worth of stories to tell her. But as much as I want time alone with Elise, this moment feels incomplete without Fatima.

"Hey, have you seen Fatima?" Elise asks. I smile because less than a minute after apologizing, we're back to reading each other's thoughts. Then I frown because I assumed Elise knew where Fatima was.

"No. And it's not like her to miss rehearsal during tech

week," I say. "Did she tell you why she couldn't give you a ride?"

"No, she just didn't show up. That's why I was late."

"Weird." I stare at Elise. Her furrowed brow matches mine. "I can check, but I actually don't think I heard from her all weekend. Which is doubly weird. The last time we texted was Thursday."

I remember it clearly, actually. I told her about my conversation with Mom and Grandma Ruby, and then Fatima randomly texted, "I'm so excited!" I assumed she was talking about the musical, but . . .

"Oh no." Elise's eyes widen.

It hits me a second later.

"Her half-birthday," I whisper. "We were supposed to plan the party."

THE LATE-SURPRISE-APOLOGY-HALF-BIRTHDAY PARTY

"No, no, no, no." Elise is pacing in front of the mirrors, clutching her cell phone. "This isn't happening."

"Try calling her again."

"She's not answering."

"Okay, I'll try." I pull out my phone and scroll through the recent call log. Fatima is all the way at the bottom. I press the sweaty device to my ear and wait as it rings and rings and . . . clicks off.

"It only rang twice. Does that mean she refused the call? Or is something wrong with my phone?"

"She's mad." Elise sighs. "How in the world did we let this happen?"

"Well, you were angry at me and then I was angry at you and then—"

"I know how it happened," Elise snaps. "I was being rhetorical."

"Sorry." I slide my phone back into my pocket. "I was trying to help."

"I know. Sorry."

A brief pause extends into awkward silence. Elise and I haven't spoken in weeks. Sure, we technically both apologized, but this friendship feels fragile. Like the tiniest misunderstanding could blow up our temporary peace. And somehow, I was so busy hating Elise that I accidentally destroyed another relationship in the process. Which totally sucks. This was supposed to be the best summer ever, and it's turning into the summer where Shannon ruins her whole life.

"It's not too late," Elise says. "It's only, what . . . ?" She looks at her phone. "Three o'clock! We'll get some food, buy a cake, and surprise Fatima at her house. It'll be, like, a part apology, part half-birthday party. What do you think?"

I think we missed Fatima's half-birthday and it's too late and she'll probably hate us forever. But I push the thought aside. If I've learned anything, it's that doing something is better than doing nothing, even when that something is risky and awkward and scary. Instead, I nod and tap my elbows three times each. I need a little bit of good luck now more than ever.

"I'm in."

"Great." Elise starts throwing stuff into an oversized tote bag and putting on her normal clothes. Once I locate my shorts, I change too. "We can go to the grocery store near her house for cake and stuff," Elise says. "My dads are at work, but maybe your mom can take us?"

"Yeah, sure." Then I remember what Mom said in the car. "Wait, no. She and my grandma are meeting with builder people. I was supposed to get a ride home." I frown. "What do we do?"

"Amir?" Elise asks.

"Didn't he not pick you up this morning because Fatima was mad? Why would he help us now?"

"Because *now* we're throwing his sister a late-surprise-apology-half-birthday party." Elise grins. "And he can't leave us here. That's probably illegal or something."

We abandon our costumes in rumpled piles—that's a problem for tomorrow—grab our backpacks, and run into the auditorium. Sure enough, Amir and Naomi are still onstage, working through a scene. We hover in the wings until it looks like they're finishing up.

"Amir, wait!" Elise calls.

He turns around, narrows his eyes when he sees it's us, then hops off the stage and starts walking up the aisle.

"Amir, please!" We both run after him. "We're sorry we forgot Fatima's half-birthday. You have to help us!"

He keeps walking.

"We want to get her a cake and throw her a party," I say. "Come on. Aren't you supposed to be acting like our father? Wouldn't a father want to help his daughters?"

I can see Amir hesitate, but he doesn't give in yet. His loyalty to Fatima is admirable, though slightly annoying.

"Also, neither of us has a ride," Elise says. "So if you leave us here, we might get kidnapped, and that probably wouldn't look good on college applications. If you were, like, the reason two innocent twelve-year-olds die."

Amir groans and spins around. "Fine, just hurry up." Elise and I high-five. "I was never actually going to leave without you."

Our celebratory mood dampens when Amir spends the entire drive to the grocery store explaining all the ways we broke Fatima's heart. According to him, his sister spent an hour crying, another hour attempting (and failing) to bake scones, and the next three hours playing K-pop in her bedroom at an earsplitting volume.

"She's such a *sad* crier," he says. "And I couldn't have friends over because she was blasting music. It was unbearable."

"What was unbearable?" Elise asks. "Your little sister being sad or you not having friends over?"

"And isn't everyone *technically* a sad crier?" I ask.

"Children, children, children," he says, once again using his formal Captain von Trapp voice. Elise and I smile at each other. At least Amir has forgiven us. And hopefully, Fatima can be persuaded with cake.

When we reach the grocery store, Amir offers us his wallet, but Elise shoos him away. "We've got it," she says confidently.

"We do?" I ask, thinking of the three single dollar bills in my own wallet.

"We do. I have a debit card for emergencies."

"Um, but we're buying a cake."

"Yeah, an *emergency* cake."

The grocery store is packed, so we split up. Elise heads for the bakery section, and I steer my cart toward the snack aisle, looking for anything and everything Fatima might enjoy. I grab Double Stuf OREOs, her all-time favorite snack food. Nilla Wafers, which we built castles with back in first grade. And a giant bag of Twizzlers because they remind me of working concessions with Fatima during previous shows.

I'm getting a stomachache just looking at my cart, though, so I move to the fresh food section next. I get a bag of kiwis to represent the science project we did together on the ecosystem of kiwi birds. A boxed sushi roll from the refrigerator case because Fatima has been begging me to try sushi for years. And a bag of organic pears because of a ridiculous inside joke we have about pears and parrots.

Looking at the seemingly random pile of food almost makes me cry. It's like seeing the history of our friendship in a single grocery cart. And if these snacks are enough to make me tear up, I'm hopeful they'll soften Fatima's anger too.

I pull myself together and push the cart back across the store. Elise is standing in line at the bakery counter, behind someone picking up a huge number of soccer-themed cupcakes.

"I'm thinking chocolate." Elise points to a large sheet cake in the glass display case.

"Sounds good. How are my snack choices?"

"Absolutely perfect." Elise smiles as she surveys the cart. "Please tell me this sushi is for you. Oh, and the kiwi project! I loved that one. And the parrot named Pear! She's going to—"

"Next!" the woman behind the counter barks, jolting me and Elise back to reality. The guy with the soccer cupcakes is long gone.

"Hi, yes." Elise steps up the counter. "We'd like a chocolate cake." She points to the sprinkle-covered one in the case. "And can you write something on it?"

"What do you want it to say?"

"Um . . ." Elise chews on the inside of her cheek. "How about, 'Happy half-birthday, Fatima! Also, sorry.' And the name is spelled F-A-T-I-M-A." Elise gives the woman her brightest smile, but the exhausted bakery worker just sighs and jots the message onto a notepad.

"All right," she says. "When do you need it?"

"Um, now?" Elise tries.

"We can't do that," the woman says. "Tomorrow morning is the earliest it can be ready."

Elise and I exchange a look. By tomorrow, Fatima may have given up on us. And we can't force Amir to spend another night listening to K-pop after driving us halfway across the city.

"We'll take the cake plain," I say. To Elise I whisper, "I've got a plan."

• • • • • •

"If you get any icing in my car, I will disown both of you," Amir says.

"We're being careful," I say, even though there are already sprinkles scattered across the backseat. Elise covers her mouth with one hand to avoid laughing. With the other hand, she's holding our cake steady on the armrest.

"Okay, do you trust me?" I ask.

"Absolutely," Elise says. I was asking about my vision for decorating the cake, but when I see the kind expression on my friend's face, I realize her answer meant so much more.

I squeeze her hand, then pull the Double Stuf OREOs out of the shopping bag. I rip open the plastic container and grab a bunch of cookies. The chocolate dust immediately coats my palms and slips under my fingernails. Dirty hands are almost as uncomfortable as dirty feet, but I remind myself that I'm doing this for Fatima. Also, I have sanitizer in my backpack.

I arrange the OREOs into numbers. First a one, then a two. I had planned on using a fraction—we're celebrating a half-birthday, after all—but the cake isn't that big once it's covered in cookies. Instead, I use a single OREO as a decimal point and add one more number so the cake reads 12.5.

"It's perfect," Elise says.

"But will it work?" I ask.

"We'll see soon enough."

When we arrive at Fatima's house, Amir parks in the garage and lets himself in through the kitchen door. Elise and I trail behind him.

"Fatima!" He dumps his bag on the table and grabs a Mountain Dew from the fridge. "Your former friends are here!"

"That's not helping," I whisper.

Amir grins before disappearing into the basement. Elise and I walk slowly into the pristine living room. She's still holding the cake, and I'm still holding our bag full of snacks. We pause in front of the giant family portrait that hangs above the fireplace.

"Should we call for her again or just go upstairs?" I look to Elise, who shrugs.

I'm about to take my chances and shout, when a door creaks open. Moments later, Fatima appears at the top of the stairs. She's wearing gray sweatpants and a gray sweatshirt—an obvious I-haven't-gotten-out-of-bed-all-day outfit—and her arms are crossed.

"You two better have a good apology," she says. Then, a moment later, "And that better be a cake."

L ast year, two best friends in our grade got into a massive fight. Grace and Faith—yes, those are *really* their names—went from spending every second of the day together to being mortal enemies. I didn't know what they were arguing about. Honestly, I'm not sure Grace and Faith even knew. There were shady pictures posted on Instagram, a sabotaged science fair project, horrible rumors spread around school, and a very public fight on the playground that involved hair-pulling and dirt-throwing.

After the playground incident, the principal made Grace and Faith meet together with the guidance counselor before they were allowed back in school. Kinda like couple's counseling, but for friends. According to Grace, they did trust exercises and art therapy and talked about their problems while the counselor watched and asked questions.

That's what we need right now. A bunch of coloring books and a trained professional. Instead, we have a bag of food, a half-birthday cake, and a goldfish named Harry.

"Harry looks happy." Elise peers into the fishbowl on Fatima's dresser.

"Harry is a goldfish," Fatima says. "Their only moods are happy and dead."

The three of us are sitting in a perfect triangle on Fatima's blue shag rug. In contrast to the rest of the house, her room is its usual mess. There are clothes dumped everywhere, a poster dangling from the wall by a single pushpin, and a trash can overflowing with candy wrappers and browning apple cores. Last year, Fatima's parents decided to stop nagging her about cleaning her room. They thought she might eventually grow tired of living in a pigsty and learn to clean it herself. So far, that hasn't happened.

I push a pile of laundry—clean or dirty is anyone's guess—out of my way and arrange the snacks. Elise takes the lid off our cake and places it between us. I can see recognition dawning in Fatima's eyes as she looks at our measly selection of gifts. A smile pulls at the edge of her mouth.

"Omigod, you guys." Fatima buries her face in her hands. "This is so cute."

"Isn't that a good thing?" I ask.

"No! I want to be mad!" Fatima wails. "You two were so busy fighting that you forgot my half-birthday. Even though you promised to plan something. Even though I reminded you a billion times." My face grows warm, and I stare at my bare legs. "But I suck at staying angry. Because you brought me all this food and the most hideous cake I've ever seen . . ."

"Hey now," I say in mock protest, though I have to admit Fatima has a point. Despite my expertly placed OREO cookies, the cake is looking a little grim. During our backseat decorating session, one corner got super squished and a bunch of sprinkles fell off.

". . . and I don't want to be mad," Fatima continues. "I want to eat this entire cake with you guys and watch Harry swim in circles."

"That sounds good to me," Elise says.

"But I'm mad!" Fatima balls up the receipt from the shopping bag and chucks it toward me. Except her aim isn't great, so it lands in the center of the cake. I can't help it. I burst into laughter. So does Elise. Fatima holds out for a minute, but then she's laughing too.

"Okay, here's my plan," I say as we calm down. "You start eating the hideous cake while we tell you how sorry we are." Elise opens the box of plastic forks and hands them over. Fatima takes a massive bite of cake and motions for us to talk.

"I'll go first," Elise says. "I am so, so, so, so, *so* sorry I forgot your half-birthday. And that I've been a terrible friend all summer. And that I started the whole thing with Shannon in the first place." Fatima nods at each of these points. I feel a tiny bit validated that Elise admitted to starting all the drama between us. "And I hope you forgive me and we can be friends again."

Fatima points her crumb-covered fork at me. "Now you."

"Um, well . . ." Elise covered the main points. "I'm sorry for all the same things, really." I try to think of something different, so Fatima knows I'm sincere. "I think I've been so worried about myself that I forgot what was most important. Which is you guys. So I'm sorry."

There's a super long pause as Fatima takes another bite of cake. In his bowl, Harry does two full laps around the plastic castle.

Eventually, Fatima breaks the silence. "Well, I officially accept your apologies." She grins. "Thank god. It is so stressful being angry. I swear I got a bunch of pimples from crying all weekend." Fatima hands both of us forks so we can dig in too. "Seriously, how did you two stay mad for so long? If it hadn't been so annoying, I might be impressed."

Elise and I exchange an uneasy look. The fact that we hated each other for most of the summer is pretty pathetic.

Especially considering it only took Fatima five minutes to forgive both of us.

"Wait a minute." Fatima looks back and forth between us. "You two *did* make up, right? You talked about your feelings and cried and hugged and all that jazz?"

"We apologized," I say.

"And hugged," Elise says.

"And I cried. But that was more because I couldn't find any ChapStick." That reminds me. I pull out a blue tube—thanks to Elise, I now have two—and apply the ChapStick while Fatima glares at us.

"You have to actually talk about your feelings," she says. "You know, discuss *why* you were fighting. Work out your issues."

I stare at the floor. I'm not sure what to say to Elise. Partly because I feel seriously awkward and partly because I'm still not sure *exactly* why she was mad at me. A counselor and coloring books would definitely come in handy right about now.

"Oh, for Pete's sake," Fatima says, sounding exactly like Grandma Ruby. She stands up and retrieves Harry from her dresser. Then she carefully sits back down, holding the fishbowl between her legs. "If you can't talk to each other, talk to Harry. He's great at keeping secrets. Though he will silently judge you."

I laugh a little, then stare into his glassy fish eyes. "Okay, *Harry*. I'm obviously very sorry for everything I said to Elise in the bathroom at Adeline's house. I didn't mean any of that stuff. Well, maybe I did a tiny bit. But only because I was so angry and confused. The truth is I was devastated when Elise stopped talking to me. I didn't understand."

The room is silent except for the hum of the air conditioner and Fatima crunching on an OREO. Finally, Elise talks.

"You were right in the bathroom," she says softly. "I was jealous." I jerk my head to look at Elise, but her eyes are trained on Harry. "It didn't seem fair. I've worked so hard to improve my singing and dancing, and you waltz in and get an amazing part when you weren't even trying."

"But I—"

"Let her talk," Fatima says to me.

"You're so good at everything," Elise says. "You get perfect grades in school and you're good at making friends and boys like you and . . . and I just wanted this one thing." Elise's voice is growing stronger, and I can't tell if she's about to scream or cry. "My dads paid for private voice lessons for me all spring. Because I begged them to. Because I desperately wanted to get better. And then I totally blew my audition, which sucked. And then you get onstage and you're everything I want to be! Without even trying or caring!" Elise chokes back a sob. "So yeah, I was jealous. And I wanted a break from hanging out with you because I was scared of saying everything I just said. So when we started arguing in the bathroom . . ."

". . . I said everything you already felt bad about, which made you feel a million times worse."

"Yeah." Elise is still looking at Harry.

"I'm sorry," I say.

"No." She shakes her head. "I mean, yes. But if you're sorry, I'm five times sorrier. It was my problem, and I took it out on you."

Fatima holds up the fishbowl and looks her orange and white pet straight in the eyes. "We did it, Harry! We're geniuses!"

Elise and I laugh, but I'm amazed by Fatima. It took Grace and Faith three sessions with a guidance counselor. And counselors go to college for this sort of thing. All Fatima needed was a goldfish.

"If it makes you feel any better, I can tell you plenty of things I'm bad at."

"Oh yeah?" Elise shoves a giant hunk of chocolate cake into her mouth. She's no longer using the fork. "Actually, that would help. What things?"

"Well . . . I got an eighty-eight in science last semester."

"That's a good grade!" Elise shouts, flicking a crumb at me.

"Um . . . I lied to my therapist for half the summer. And I had a meltdown about ChapStick earlier today."

"Those are both because of your OCD," Fatima says. "That doesn't count."

"Okay." I search my brain. "Ooh, I've got it. I've been trying to work up the nerve to ask Micah if he wants to be my boyfriend, but I keep chickening out. And that's not because of the OCD. That's just because I'm pathetic."

"You two still haven't talked about that?" Fatima rolls her eyes.

"Nooo!" Elise flops onto the floor and pulls a pillow over her face.

"What?" I ask. "Don't tell me you like him too. Because you can have him. I'm not that invested."

And I'm not losing you again, I think.

"No, I'm mad at myself for missing so much this summer," she says. "Naomi and Adeline are so boring. All they do is talk about college. I need all the real gossip now."

For the next hour, Elise, Fatima, Harry, and I hang out on the rug. The humans consume half the chocolate cake—fitting for a half-birthday—while Harry swims in circles and nibbles on fish food. Elise wants details about every single interaction between me and Micah. She tells us about the messiness that is the love triangle between Amir, Naomi, and Adeline. And Fatima confirms, based on top-secret intel from Mrs. Davis, that she and Mr. Bryant are officially an item.

Once we're in that familiar, giggly state that comes from eating too much sugar, we switch to the healthy food. Fatima and Elise gang up on me and force me to eat a piece of sushi (which is revolting), and we tell the Pear-y the Parrot joke until our sides hurt from laughing. Fatima is trying to convince us she can peel a kiwi with her toes when the doorbell rings.

"I should see who it is," Fatima says. "Amir never hears anything in the basement."

We follow Fatima down the stairs and peek through the blinds in a totally not-subtle way, in case there's a murderer waiting outside the door. When we see Mr. Bryant's bald head, we laugh even more. Fatima swings open the door.

"Hey, what are you doing here?" she asks through giggles.

Mr. Bryant steps inside like he's been here a thousand times, which he probably has. He's good friends with Mr. and Mrs. Suleiman. "Amir left half his possessions backstage in the dressing room." He holds up a laptop, a backpack, and a bunch of cords. "I figured he'd want his computer before tomorrow, so I thought I'd drop it off."

"Oh, cool. He's in the basement. You can—"

Right then, the loudest scream I've ever heard pierces through the house. Which is pretty darn loud when you consider how much noise Elise, Fatima, and I were making upstairs. Before we can react, there's another scream.

Elise clutches my hand.

Mr. Bryant nearly drops the computer.

"Amir!" Fatima yells.

In unison, we all turn toward the basement and run.

THE SHOW MUST GO ON

We race down the stairs. Fatima reaches the bottom first. She ignores the Do Not Enter sign on the closed door and bursts into the basement. Elise, Mr. Bryant, and I are right behind her.

I don't know what I expected to see. Maybe a puddle of blood or vomit. Or an intruder wearing a ski mask. Or a giant, hairy spider. It certainly sounded like the scream of someone whose life was in danger. Instead, we find a shirtless Amir, sitting cross-legged in a beanbag chair, staring at his cell phone, and grinning from ear to ear.

"Are you okay?" Fatima rushes to his side, still terrified.

Amir shrieks in response. Now that I can see his face, though, I realize it's a sound of delight.

"Are you serious?" Fatima punches him in the arm and not particularly lightly. "What happened? I thought you were dying or something. We all did." She gestures to the little crowd hovering in the doorway. Amir looks up, noticing our presence for the first time.

I tentatively step inside and peer around the open room. I've been to Fatima's house a hundred times, but I've never stepped foot in the basement Amir claimed as his bedroom. He has a strict "no visitors" policy. Which is a shame because his whole setup is amazing. On one wall, he has a TV with a bunch of video game consoles attached. On the opposite wall, there's an unmade queen-sized bed. And everywhere in between, there are shelves of books and scripts and playbills and stacks of loose papers. But it's not chaotic like Fatima's bedroom. I can tell from the handwritten labels on each shelf that Amir has a detailed organizational system.

Mr. Bryant clears his throat and steps farther into the room. "You okay, Amir? You scared us half to death."

"Yeah, sorry," Amir says, though his grin is anything but sorry.

"So what happened?" Fatima asks. "You can't screech like that and then be all mysterious."

"Okay, do you remember that preprofessional intensive I applied for in New York City?" Amir asks. It takes me a second to remember what he's talking about. It feels like forever ago that Fatima was telling us about Amir's big-city dreams, but it was just last month.

"Yeah, and?"

"Well, I didn't get in. I knew that already. But there's a director who's interested in meeting me!" He holds up his phone, not that any of us can read it from across the room. "She saw my audition tape and wants to fly me to New York for a reading. Like a legit reading, with professionals and everything."

"Omigod." Fatima's mouth drops open.

"Congratulations, man!" Mr. Bryant is beaming.

"What's the show?" Elise asks.

"And when do you leave?" I ask.

"I don't know," Amir says. "I started screaming before I finished reading the email."

"Well, then finish reading the email, genius!" Fatima punches his arm again.

"Okay, um . . ." Amir scans his screen. "Saw the video . . . new musical . . . fly to New York City . . . Oh." His face falls.

"What?!" we all yell at once.

The excitement that was radiating from Amir moments ago is gone. "It's this weekend," he says finally. "They want me to come this weekend."

"But our show opens this weekend," I say, stating the obvious.

"I know." Amir throws his phone across the room. It bounces off a stack of papers and lands, thankfully, on a pillow. "What am I supposed to do?" He hugs his knees to his chest and presses his face against his knees. "What am I supposed to do?!"

"Hey. Amir. Listen to me." Mr. Bryant strides across the room. Fatima jumps out of the way to make room next to the beanbag chair. "It's obvious what you do, okay? There's only one choice here."

"Yeah?" Amir looks up.

"Of course," Mr. Bryant says. I'm expecting him to say something adult-sounding like honoring your commitments or not giving up on your team, but he doesn't. "You get on a plane to New York. This is the real world. This is your career. There's no way I'm letting you miss a professional opportunity for our musical. We'll figure it out."

"But how?" Amir asks. I'm thinking the exact same thing. He has the second-biggest part in the entire show. And he doesn't have an understudy because there weren't enough boys at auditions. Not that most guys could handle the part anyway.

"We'll figure something out," Mr. Bryant says. "You don't need to worry."

The rest of us do need to worry, though.

We move our meeting upstairs to the kitchen. Elise and I both call our parents and tell them we're spending the night at Fatima's house. Mr. Bryant calls Mrs. Davis, who comes over right away. Naomi and Adeline are close behind her, their arms heavy with massive bags of takeout.

Amir stayed downstairs to call his parents, and we can hear his shrieks of excitement from the kitchen. Mr. and Mrs. Suleiman aren't typical stage parents, but they've always been Amir's biggest fans. They're sure to be overjoyed. Our show may be falling apart, but it's falling apart because of good news. That's something, at least.

Fatima drags in a couple chairs from the dining room so we all fit around the table. We pile our plates with Thai food—even those of us who spent the last two hours devouring half a chocolate cake—and look to Mr. Bryant for direction. He is the director, after all. But he's staring blankly out the window, drumming his fingers on the table.

"Ned, honey, tell us what you're thinking," Mrs. Davis says.

Fatima gives me and Elise an I-told-you-so look.

"I'm thinking I should have cast understudies. That was a bad decision." Mr. Bryant pounds his fist against the table. "There are a handful of kids in the chorus who could have done it. But now it's too late. Nobody can learn that entire part in less than a week."

"So what do we do?" Adeline asks. "Can we delay opening night?"

"Nope." Mr. Bryant shakes his head. "We've already sold tickets."

"Can we pay an actual actor?" Elise asks. "Like the theater downtown is doing?"

"Even if they could learn the part, we don't have the budget," Mr. Bryant says.

The room grows silent as everyone ponders our dilemma. I still think Elise's idea could work. We just need somebody who (1) already knows the part, (2) is available next weekend, and (3) would be generous enough to help for free. If only we had the same budget as Northern Rep.

"Wait, I've got it!" Everyone turns to face me. "The other theater is doing *The Sound of Music* too. And they're really good, right? You've been talking about them all summer."

"I don't know if this is helpful," Naomi says.

"No, listen! My point is that *they* might have an understudy for Captain von Trapp. What if we borrowed him? I know we don't have money, but we could promote their theater at intermission or something."

"You're a genius," Fatima says.

"See, I knew you were good at everything," Elise says.

"It was your idea first," I say, but I'm blushing from all the praise. Being the person who saves the day feels really freaking good.

We all watch as Mr. Bryant types furiously on his cell phone. My legs are bouncing with nervous energy while I tap my elbows. After all of our hard work, after all of the drama, I can't imagine *not* being Brigitta.

Mr. Bryant updates us periodically: "I've got the number of the director."

A few minutes later: "I explained the situation to her."

Then: "Okay, there's a text bubble! She's replying."

And finally: "Okay, okay, okay!" He bites his lip. "Yes!"

"What?!" Mrs. Davis jumps up. "Do they have someone for us?"

"Yup." Mr. Bryant is beaming. "Jared Tolbert. He's a junior at Fountain High School, and he's been understudying for Captain von Trapp this entire summer!" He pauses to read as more messages come through. "*And* he's excited to work with us. *And* he'll be at our rehearsals starting on Monday!"

The kitchen fills with cheers. Fatima, Elise, and I are hugging each other. Naomi and Adeline are dancing around the table. Mr. Bryant and Mrs. Davis sneak a kiss when they think nobody's looking. I'm so busy laughing and celebrating and thanking the theater gods for Jared what's-his-name that I don't hear Amir enter the kitchen.

"Did you hear?" Fatima yells over the commotion. "There's a kid—" My best friend stops talking and her face falls.

I spin around to see Amir slumped in a kitchen chair, his forehead resting on the table. And just like that, the celebrating stops. I glance around the room, but everyone looks as confused as me. If anything, this is extra good news for Amir. Now he doesn't have to feel guilty about abandoning the show.

"Amir, what's going on?" Fatima rushes to her brother's side. "Talk to me."

"I can't go to New York." His voice is barely louder than a whisper.

"What? Why?" Mr. Bryant slides into the seat next to him.

"My parents have a catering job next weekend. They can't miss it." Amir takes a shaky breath. "And they said I can't fly to New York by myself."

"But you have to," Fatima says.

"Surely there's another way," Mr. Bryant says.

"They said the only option was . . ." Amir shakes his head. "Never mind."

"What?!" Now Naomi and Adeline are huddled around him too. "What's the option?"

Amir sits up slowly. All his giddiness is gone. "They said I could go to New York if I found a chaperone to come with me. Someone they trusted. Someone like Mr. Bryant."

"I can—"

"No!" Amir barely lets our director get a word out. "There's no way I can ask you to do that. It's bad enough that you suddenly need an understudy, but this show won't happen without you." He sighs. "There will be other opportunities. It's not the right time."

"But I want—"

"I know you want to help." Amir stares at his hands. "But Mrs. Davis can't do everything by herself. Especially if someone new is taking over my part."

"We would need an understudy director," I say softly, and Amir nods.

The energy in Fatima's kitchen deflates like a popped balloon. Of course, everyone wants Amir to go to New York. But it's impossible to argue with his logic. Mr. Bryant chaperoning would mean leaving behind a cast and crew of over one hundred kids.

It's not just the people gathered around this table. There are more than a dozen nuns who have worked super hard, even if they're still kinda terrible. The boys who spent weeks practicing marching like soldiers. There are kids doing props and costumes and lighting. Everyone both onstage and off has sacrificed their time and energy to make this musical a success.

"So what do we do now?" Naomi asks.

"Pretend none of this ever happened." Amir's voice cracks, and I worry he's about to start crying. Adeline reaches out and squeezes his hand.

"Actually, I might have a solution," Fatima says. She's been silent this whole time, picking at her plate of plain rice as Amir's dreams of being on Broadway get crushed.

"You know an understudy director?" Elise asks.

"Maybe." Fatima glances at me with an apologetic shrug. "I've been talking to Shannon's grandmother some, and—"

"YOU'VE BEEN WHAT?!?"

Fatima has met Grandma Ruby exactly twice. Once at Valley Fair and once when we were running lines. Have they been chatting all this time without me knowing?

"Well, she knows a lot about theater," Fatima says. "And she was super helpful when we ran into problems with the costumes."

"Yeah, she was great during our rehearsal," Naomi adds. "She basically blocked the entire thing. No offense, Mr. Bryant."

"Oh, none taken." Our director laughs. "I'm a big fan of Ms. Carter."

I'm still staring at Fatima, shocked by her revelation. I feel slightly betrayed that she and Grandma Ruby have been secretly discussing costume design. But mostly, I'm amused. My best friend and my grandmother becoming friends is the last thing I expected to happen this summer.

"What are you saying?" There's a glimmer of hope in Amir's voice.

"I'm saying she can direct," Fatima says. "Well, she can help Mrs. Davis direct. Then Mr. Bryant can go to New York, and Amir can go to his reading. I know it's not ideal, but the show must go on, right? We can at least ask."

FRO-YO

Grandma Ruby says yes.

As if there was any chance she would say no. The opportunity to boss people around *and* relive her glory days? That's basically her dream come true.

Mr. Bryant and Amir don't leave until Thursday, but Grandma Ruby is so eager to take charge that Mr. Bryant lets her start right away. He says it's to help her transition, but I think he's secretly scared of my grandmother.

I have to admit that Fatima was spot-on. Grandma Ruby is a natural at readjusting blocking and cleaning up choreography, which gives Mr. Bryant time to work with the new Captain von Trapp. Jared may not be Amir, but he's pretty darn good.

Grandma Ruby—of course—decides to make a bunch of changes, something Mr. Bryant would never do so close to opening night. She eliminates most of the jumping and dancing in the bedroom scene because our breath control is "simply abysmal." Brigitta's conversation with Maria gets sped up because our pacing reminds her of "watching paint dry on a humid day." And she moves Sara and Riya front and center for most of our scenes. According to her, their general cuteness will distract the audience from any mistakes the rest of the cast makes.

On Thursday, we say goodbye to Mr. Bryant and Amir, then head straight to the theater for our final dress rehearsal. We're running the show from start to finish in full costume and makeup, and we can't call for lines or stop the show for any reason. "If someone breaks their arm, find a way to make it work," Grandma Ruby says.

During our previous dress rehearsals, I wore my normal zip-up boots with my costume. It was easy to forget about my shoe situation because some kids were still going barefoot or wearing tennis shoes. But today, everyone is wearing the filthy character shoes I refuse to touch. I zip up my own boots, feeling extra nervous.

The dress rehearsal is almost perfect. In fact, it's so perfect the older kids start freaking out. When I ask why, Naomi stares at me like I asked what color the sky was.

"It's the rule," she explains, sounding panicked. "A bad dress rehearsal means the show will be great. So a good dress rehearsal . . ." Naomi raises her eyebrows.

"Means the show will be horrible?" Micah finishes for her.

"Exactly."

"I don't know," I say. "That kinda sounds like something people say to reassure themselves when a dress rehearsal sucks."

"Oh, it definitely is," Elise whispers. "But I wouldn't argue with actors about their superstitions." We both laugh at Naomi, who is now pacing in circles backstage.

"Hey, I was going to ask if you and Fatima want to sleep over tonight," Elise says. "Since our last sleepover wasn't so great." I grimace at the memory of that awkward night. It feels like an eternity ago—before I was even cast as Brigitta.

"Absolutely," I say. "We deserve a do-over. I need to talk to Grandma Ruby first, though. Ask her about my shoes." I pull up the bottom of my skirt to reveal my zip-up boots.

Elise smiles sympathetically and wishes me luck.

I find Grandma Ruby studying a legal pad in the audience. The yellow pages are covered in her tiny, messy cursive, and she's flipping between them, circling notes, and drawing arrows from one thing to the next. This is where my grandmother was meant to be. Not stuck in my bedroom with nothing to do, but leading a massive cast and crew.

"Hey, Grandma." I plop into the seat next to her. "I'm

going to sleep over at Elise's tonight. So I won't see you until call tomorrow."

"Mmm-hmm." She barely looks up from her notes.

That isn't what I needed to say. I fiddle with my costume, not sure how to bring up my shoe problem. Two months ago, I never would have mentioned my OCD to Grandma Ruby. But she understands me better now. I understand her better too.

"You know how I only wear three pairs of shoes?" I go for the direct approach.

Grandma Ruby looks up, startled to find me still sitting next to her. "I am aware."

"Well, I meant to ask Mr. Bryant before he left, but I can't put those dirty character shoes on my feet. But if I wear these, they won't match." I lift my leg in the air to show her the offending boots. "Are you worried about that?"

"Shannon." She places her hand stiffly on my leg. This kind of affection is entirely new for us, but I don't mind.

"I am worried your friend Elise won't hit the right note in the last stanza of 'Do-Re-Mi.' I am worried the lighting cues in the finale are too obviously joyful. I am worried about the microphones Evelyn promised to fix but hasn't yet. I am worried about a great many things, my dear. Your shoes are not one of them. Just slap some black tape over the zipper, and you've got boots from the 1930s."

"How did I not think of that?" I stare in awe at my grandmother.

"It's nothing to fret about," Grandma Ruby says. "I have years of experience with this sort of thing. You know, when I was in that critically acclaimed production of *Guys and Dolls* . . ."

Mom insists on driving me to Elise's house.

While she hums along to the radio, a faint smile playing at her lips, I stare at my reflection in the tiny mirror. I tried to wash off my stage makeup before leaving the theater, but my eyes and cheeks are still smudged with black mascara. I look like I spent the last hour sobbing, not singing and dancing.

Mom doesn't turn into Elise's subdivision. Instead, she keeps driving and makes a left into the parking lot of a high-end strip mall. Small clusters of teenagers are wandering between stores while older couples in formal clothing wait for dinner reservations.

"Um, hello? You're supposed to be taking me to Elise's house?"

"We'll get there eventually." Mom pulls into a parking space next to the Yogurt Factory, the fancier of the two fro-yo chains in our suburb. "Surely I'm allowed to celebrate my daughter's stage debut?"

"Mo-om! I can't go in there." As much as frozen yogurt sounds delicious, I look ridiculous.

"What? Are you already too much of a teenager to be seen with your mother?"

"Do you see my face? What if I see somebody I know? I look like a raccoon!"

"Yes, but a very cute raccoon." Mom shifts the car into park and opens her door. "Come on. Humor me."

After a quick stop in the bathroom to wash my hands and scrub my cheeks one more time, I join Mom in the fro-yo line. She's balancing three different sample cups with unusual flavors like Pineapple Guava and Peanut Butter Crackers. I fill a bowl with plain vanilla yogurt, then move on to the toppings bar, where I choose chopped strawberries. As usual, I have to wait at the cash register while Mom fills her bowl with five different flavors and every topping imaginable, from Lucky Charms to Skittles. Anyone looking at our bowls would guess that she was the twelve-year-old, not me.

I pick a small table in the back of the restaurant. I know rationally that nobody is staring at my smeared makeup, but I feel better with a bit of privacy. Mom takes a huge bite of her yogurt. My stomach turns as I imagine her five different flavors (and twenty-five toppings) mixing together.

"Are you ready for opening night?" Mom asks.

"Yup." I take a bite of my own fro-yo. "I talked to Grandma Ruby about my shoe problem, and she had the perfect solution."

"Of course she did." Mom laughs a little. "You know . . . I was really concerned about you doing this musical."

"Oh no." I groan. "We've been over this a million times." I glare at my mom. Did she really bring me to the Yogurt Factory to persuade me to quit? Less than twenty-four hours before opening night? I thought we solved this problem with the Talking Napkin Ring.

"No, no. Hear me out." Mom points her spoon at me. A piece of Kit Kat falls onto the table, and I quickly wipe it away with a napkin. "I *was* concerned about you doing the musical. Even more than I let on, probably. Some nights, I had trouble sleeping because I was so afraid for you. Putting yourself out there, trying something new—that's a big deal for anybody, but especially someone like you."

"Aw, Mom. I'm really okay."

"I know." She takes a shaky breath. "I really do know that, Shannon. I guess . . ." Mom trails off as she takes another bite. It's a full minute before she speaks again. "Do you remember when we lived in the apartment? Every night, you would count the roses on your sheets for hours."

I nod, because I do remember. Mom reading me books while I counted myself to sleep. My pink lamp casting a warm glow on the beige wallpaper. My bare feet rubbing against the scratchy sheets. There were times when the sun would rise before I finally drifted off to sleep. But when I woke up the next afternoon—sometimes having missed an entire day of school—Mom would still be next to me, stroking my hair.

"I was terrified of doing something wrong. I thought..." Mom chokes on her words. "You seemed so breakable back then. I thought if I changed your sheets or read the wrong story, you might shatter into a million pieces."

Mom wipes a tear from her cheeks. I can feel my own eyes stinging. I knew things were difficult when I was younger—this was before I had any medication or therapy—but I didn't know how much it affected my mom.

"I'm sorry." My voice is small.

"No, no. You don't need to be sorry. That's not what I'm saying." Mom scoops a massive spoonful of fro-yo into her mouth. She takes a moment to swallow, but then she's smiling again. "My point is that *I'm* sorry. I've been underestimating you all summer. In my head, you're still that little girl who can't stop counting roses. But you're so much stronger than I give you credit for."

"Thanks." I chew on the last of my strawberries. I'm certainly more capable than I was as a little kid, but I still have plenty of rough days. I recall all the times I've freaked out about ChapStick or dirty feet this summer. "I think maybe I'm still a little breakable. That's not great."

"Eh, we're all a little breakable," Mom says. "What matters is that we can put ourselves back together again. And that we have people to help."

OPENING NIGHT

On opening night, Elise, Fatima, and I arrive super early to claim our favorite corner of the girls' dressing room. Fatima is wearing black from head to toe, like all the other techies. Elise and I are wearing sweatpants and loose tank tops while we apply makeup in front of the floor-length mirror. Elise was smart enough to bring a fleece blanket from home so we can sit on the floor without touching the grimy tiles.

One of the older girls is playing Disney music on her iPhone while people sing along into hairbrushes and flip-flops. A few moms circle the room, helping with bobby pins and zippers. As a techie, I was always too busy gluing props together or searching for missing shoes to experience this part of opening night, but the energy is electric.

"I can't believe you still haven't done it." Fatima pops

a Goldfish cracker into her mouth, then another. Unlike us, she doesn't need to spend an hour putting on makeup, a fact she's mentioned multiple times. "Just ask him to be your boyfriend."

"What if he already thinks we're dating? Or what if he's not into labels or something?" I wince as I stab myself in the eye with a mascara wand. "What if he laughs at me and tells all the other boys I'm a freak? Or what if he posts the story online and it goes viral? I would be so humiliated. I would have to live in a hole in my backyard for the rest of my sad, embarrassing, pathetic life."

"Right, but the odds of that happening are, like, pretty low, don't you think?" Elise grins.

"Just do it," Fatima says. "Walk up to him and say, 'Hey, you're pretty cool, and I've liked hanging out with you. Do you want to be my boyfriend?'"

"That's so cringy."

"No, I've got it," Elise says. "You say, 'Hey, Micah. I find you super-duper attractive. If you find me super-duper attractive, how about we make it official?' Then you wink."

"No, then I go hide in the hole in my backyard."

"Come on, Shannon. It's opening night. Take a chance."

"Fine." I grab a handful of Goldfish from Fatima and get to my feet. "Only because you two aren't going to let it go." I groan as Fatima and Elise high-five.

Adeline says she saw Micah in the lobby, so I head in

that direction. I'm jogging down the dark hallway when I run straight into Grandma Ruby.

"Shannon! For Pete's sake, why are you running?" She takes in my messy tank top and sweatpants. "And why aren't you dressed yet? I want the cast backstage in fifteen minutes."

"Sorry, Grandma. I'll be fast."

I burst through the double doors into the main lobby. There are already audience members milling about, leafing through programs, and purchasing snacks. I look totally out of place in my stage makeup, but at least I'm still wearing normal clothes. I scan the crowd for Micah. I don't see him anywhere, but I do spot a familiar shade of red.

"Ariel?"

The redhead turns around. Sure enough, it's my therapist. And right behind her is Mom.

"Sorry, I forgot to tell you," Mom says. "I invited Ariel. I hope that's all right."

"Of course! I'm so happy you came." I hug each of them.

Mom and I spent over an hour at the Yogurt Factory, chatting and laughing and reminiscing. Hopefully she'll stop worrying quite so much.

"Listen, do you mind if I talk to—"

"No problem, I'll get out of your way," Ariel says.

"No, wait," I say to her. "It's actually you I want to talk to."

Mom shoots Ariel a what-do-I-know? look and gives me one more hug. "Break a leg, sweetie," she whispers. "I'm so proud of you."

Ariel waits until my mom is out of earshot before asking if I'm okay. After lying all summer and having the intense meltdown in her office, I was worried she would be mad at me. But Ariel said she would never be mad at someone for dealing with a difficult condition. We started over with the exposure therapy, but we're taking it slower this time. During my sleepover last night, I managed to wait thirty seconds before applying my ChapStick.

"So there's this boy," I say. "I like him a lot. And I'm pretty sure he likes me. Only I don't know how to ask him to be my boyfriend. What do you think?"

"I think this is a question for your mom, not your therapist," Ariel says. "Are you even allowed to have a boyfriend?"

"Oh." This is an issue I haven't considered. Mom was excited about my date with Micah at the food truck festival, so I can't imagine she'll have any objections. "Probably," I say. "But I wanted your advice."

"Why would I have advice for you?" Ariel is smiling at me like this is an amusing joke, not a serious problem.

"Because you're a therapist? Isn't giving advice kinda your job?"

"I can give you advice when you have OCD problems.

What you've got here is a middle-school problem." Ariel laughs. "I'm afraid I've never been great at talking with boys."

"That's it? I was hoping you could give me a script or—"

"Shannon?" A familiar voice cuts through the lobby. My entire body goes numb.

"Is that him?" Ariel whispers. "He's cute."

I nod, and she stares over my shoulder for way too long.

"Well, I better be finding my seat," Ariel says loudly enough for everyone in the lobby to hear.

"Wait a second!" I whisper. "You didn't give me any—" I whirl around to stop Ariel, only to find myself face to face with Micah. My therapist is halfway across the lobby. She smiles over her shoulder and gives me a thumbs-up.

"Hey there." Micah grins, and his lopsided dimples make my heart beat faster. He's already changed into his sailor costume. "I heard you were looking for me."

"I was? Uh, yeah. I mean, I was." I search my brain for a convincing lie, but nothing comes to me. "It doesn't matter now," I say.

We walk to the dressing room together, our arms swinging back and forth so our hands occasionally brush against each other. Grandma Ruby is going to freak out if I'm not in my costume pronto. I'm running out of time.

"Hey, actually, I wanted to ask you something." Every

organ in my body is seizing with embarrassment. I can't believe I'm going with Fatima's idea, but it's too late to change course now. "It's been cool hanging out with you. So I was wondering if you wanted to be my boyfriend." I pause. "Well, I should ask my mom first, but I'm pretty sure she'll say yes. So what do you say? If you don't want to, I totally—"

"Yes. A hundred times yes." Micah grabs my hand, saving me from myself. I knew I liked him for a reason. "It would be my honor."

⬤⬤⬤⬤⬤⬤

Everyone else is in full costume and makeup when I return to the dressing room. I throw my sweatpants onto the floor while my friends button my sailor outfit. I frantically tie navy-blue ribbons onto my braids.

"So?" Fatima asks. "What happened?"

"Oh, you mean with Micah?" I pretend like I have no idea what she's talking about. "It was easy. I found him in the hallway and asked him to be my boyfriend. He said yes, obviously. I don't know what you two were so worked up about."

Elise shrieks and hugs me while Fatima spritzes both of our heads with a bit more hairspray.

"Places in five minutes!" Grandma Ruby calls.

"Thank you, five," everyone in the dressing room chants back.

With our arms linked, the three of us head into the wings. Fatima tells both of us to break a leg before she scurries off to the sound booth, where she'll be for the rest of the show. Elise and I sneak onto the stage and peek through the heavy maroon curtains. It's the thing you're not supposed to do but everyone does anyway.

"I think I see my dads," Elise whispers; then she runs off to check her props.

I'm about to follow her, but I steal one more look at the audience. It's impossible to see individual faces, but I know Mom and Ariel are out there, waiting to cheer me on. At the back of the auditorium, Fatima will be prepping the booth with Mrs. Davis. Somewhere behind me, Grandma Ruby is freaking out about a missing nun or broken set piece. Halfway across the country, Amir is getting his shot in professional theater. And here I am, standing center stage, in a pleated dress and more makeup than I've ever worn in my life.

I thought I would be stressed on opening night, but I'm surprisingly calm. Arguing with friends is stressful. Talking to boys is stressful. Going to therapy is stressful. But playing a character and singing and dancing with my friends? This is the fun part.

In the hallway, there's a flurry of activity as Grandma

Ruby calls for places. In moments, the curtain will rise. A few scenes later, I'll be making my community theater debut.

I may not be superstitious like Adeline and Naomi, but I have my own rituals. I tap my left elbow three times, then my right. I take a few calming breaths, apply a thin layer of ChapStick, and then dash over to the line of von Trapp children.

It's time.

ACKNOWLEDGMENTS

You read my book! Thank you so much!

Seriously, my biggest shout-out goes to all the readers who picked up this book and (hopefully?) enjoyed it. Having the opportunity to write books for young people is such a privilege, and I'm honored that you spent time with these characters and this world.

And now for all the people I need to thank! (This is the boring part, so feel free to grab a different book right about now.)

First and foremost, my incredible editor, Alison Romig. I am so grateful you connected with this project, and I cannot thank you enough for all of your hard work in bringing Shannon's story into the world.

To my agent, Stacey Kondla—you are amazing and brilliant, and I am so lucky to have you on my side. I am ridiculously grateful that you encouraged me to rewrite this entire book (though I was somewhat stressed at the time) because I now can't imagine it any other way.

A huge thank-you to everyone in the MFAC program

at Hamline University for getting me here, but especially Swati Avasthi, who saw the very earliest versions of this book. (It's way better now, I swear.)

And to my lovely writing group—Lisa, Markelle, Katie, and Elizabeth. Our meetings are the highlight of my month, and I am so thankful for your advice, friendship, and support throughout the years.

I want to thank my family, and especially my mom, who definitely read this book more times than I did. (I highly recommend finding yourself a mother who doubles as a best friend, beta reader, and proofreader.) I'm only able to pursue this dream because of the emotional and financial support of my family, so I owe this all to them.

And, of course, I am forever grateful for the therapists and psychiatrists I've had throughout the years. Like Shannon, I have obsessive-compulsive disorder, and it's a big part of my life. But thanks to some lovely mental health professionals, a lot of therapy, and ongoing medication, I have a better understanding of how my brain works and how to live with this disorder. If you relate to me or Shannon, I highly, highly, *highly* recommend talking with a parent or teacher or doctor. Living with mental illness is hard, but there are ways to make it easier.

And, finally, thank you to my husband. I would write something kind and beautiful and thoughtful here, but he doesn't read books. (Don't worry, I still love him.)

ABOUT THE AUTHOR

Kalena Miller was raised in Texas but escaped its sweltering climate as soon as she could in favor of Minnesota. She received a BA from Carleton College and an MFA from Hamline University. Kalena lives in Maple Grove, Minnesota, with her husband and lovable, if slightly neurotic, dog. When she is not writing books for young readers, Kalena enjoys tap dancing, needle felting, and watching an embarrassing amount of reality television.

kalenamiller.com